BURIAL GROUND

"How many teeth does a human being have?"

David and I looked at each other.

"Thirty-two," we said together.

Willie nodded glumly. "Never saw one with thirty-three?"

I shook my head. "No. Why?"

"My dad had thirty-three," Willie said. "What do you think of that?"

"Thirty-three teeth?" David asked. "You mean a mutation?"

"I don't know what I mean. All I know is when he hit the steering wheel a couple of his front teeth and an eye tooth got knocked out. They picked 'em up from the floor of the car. And a bicuspid, too."

"A bicuspid?" I said, not sure where he was going. "But that's in the side of the mouth. A frontal blow . . ."

"You don't understand," Willie said and turned to me, pain showing in his face. "He had all his teeth. There wasn't any bicuspid missing."

BURIAL GROUND

AN ALAN GRAHAM MYSTERY

MALCOLM SHUMAN

AVON BOOKS ◆ NEW YORK

AVON BOOKS
A division of
The Hearst Corporation
1350 Avenue of the Americas
New York, New York 10019

First Avon Books Printing: March 1998

AVON TRADEMARK REG. U.S. PAT. OFF. AND IN OTHER COUNTRIES, MARCA REGISTRADA, HECHO EN U.S.A.

Printed in the U.S.A.

WCD 10 9 8 7 6 5 4 3 2 1

This is for Bill Haag,
archaeologist, teacher, and friend.

ACKNOWLEDGMENTS

The author wishes to thank his agent, Peter Rubie, for his tireless efforts, and his editor, Coates Bateman, for his conscientious attempts to make this the best book possible.

Finally, he is grateful to the staff of the Louisiana Division of Archaeology, whose professionalism has contributed so much to preserving the state's heritage.

■■■■In the Beginning

The old man looked out over the river, blinking in the afternoon sun. Already the light was melting the sky to gold over the muddy waters. The day was about to end, but the old man knew from the chill in his bones that an age was ending as well.

He was tired. They were all tired, those of the tribe who were left. It had been a long trek by canoe and afoot from the sand shores of the great southern water to the banks of the mighty river, and some had not survived the journey. But the journey had been necessary, something their hearts had told them must be done. A few had wanted to stay, arguing that the new white invaders, the ones who spoke English, would not understand, and that the old days of plenty, trading horses for the metal pots and guns, would never come again. The elders, though, had yearned to be buried in the lands of their birth, and so they had come here, settling on the banks of the river. And some had died here, as well.

Now, the old man knew, it was time to move again. Because the ones who spoke English did not understand, and it was not enough merely to be buried in one's soil: A man had to leave descendants so that his clan could survive. In the clan was the knowledge of the people. In the clan was survival.

As he watched, a pair of vultures spiraled up against the sun and then soared north on the hot wind. The old man sighed. There was a place not too different from this one, on the banks of another river, four or five moons to the west. Perhaps, with good fortune, they would find a home there, away from the whites. It would mean abandoning their village and the dead who were buried near it, but what choice was there?

The old man turned away and walked slowly toward camp, his mind set. If abandoning the dead was the price of the tribe's survival, so be it. He would be the first to be buried in the new homeland.

And that was how I imagined it, two hundred years later, when a man called me about a burial ground.

# ONE

"Dr. Graham, you've heard about the Tunica Treasure?"

I was seated at a hole-in-the-wall café in downtown Baton Rouge when T-Joe asked the question. It was a Friday morning in June, and from just over the levee came the heavy, mud smell of the river.

"Every archaeologist's heard about it," I said, trying to keep my voice steady. It had been one of the finds of the century in Southeastern archaeology.

T-Joe Dupont nodded and stirred his coffee, a few bits of powdered sugar from the beignets sprinkling down off his fingers to fall onto the surface of the hot drink.

"I hear the Indians sued everybody and got it back," he said.

It was midmorning and we were the only customers in the place. Most of the tourists were busy at the two gambling boats, two streets down on the river, and the legislature was finishing another turgid session at the state capitol where Huey Long was shot. But the rest of the old downtown section was as still as an abandoned movie set and just as quiet.

"Well, it was a little more complicated than that," I said, pushing my glasses back on my nose, "but, yes, that's essentially what happened."

He nodded again. Late forties with a friendly round face and brown eyes, he wore an open-necked sport shirt with stripes and faded slacks. Not many people's image of a millionaire, I thought.

"Nobody knew about the treasure until somebody dug it up and then everybody jumped in," he went on.

I wondered where this was going. He'd called me yesterday because he said he might have a job for a contract archaeologist and I'd been recommended, but he hadn't mentioned the Tunica discovery.

"Again, more or less true," I said, sipping my hot chocolate. "It was a trove of burial artifacts for the historic Tunica Indians, the greatest that's ever been found for any tribe in the Lower Mississippi Valley. Hundreds of iron and copper pots, European ceramics, native Indian pottery, muskets, and hundreds of thousands of glass beads." I shook my head, remembering the years of litigation involved. "It wasn't worth all that much as far as money goes—maybe ten or twenty thousand dollars on the artifact market—but it was the circumstances of where and how it was found. It was the sort of thing people get killed over. Fortunately, it just ended up in court."

"And it could end up in court again," he said.

"Come again?"

"If it was found on your land and the Indians laid claim. Then what?"

"They can't take away private land," I said and then felt foolish, because I knew what he was going to say next:

"Do it all the time for pipelines. Anyway, all they've got to do is tie it up in court." He shrugged. "Still, it'd be a hell of a story to be able to tell people you had something like that on your place."

I waited. T-Joe lifted his cup and squinted at me like he was making a decision.

"Look, Dr. Graham, I won't lie: I called another archaeologist first. Fellow named St. Ambrose. I got his name out of the phone book. But it didn't take five minutes for me to decide there was something I didn't like about him. Then I remembered a friend of mine who'd had to hire an archaeologist once. I called Fuzzy LaBordes and he said you did a good job for him at Bunkie."

"I'm glad. There wasn't much to it. Most of the area

had already been used for a municipal garbage dump years ago.''

"Still, he trusts you."

It was my turn to nod.

"And I trust you, too," he said finally, like he'd made up his mind. "It's something you learn in business. Especially oil. Lots of things done handshake only. Or used to be, when we had an oil industry. Well, the job changes but people don't."

I exhaled slightly. "Just what is it you trust me to do, Mr. Dupont?"

"T-Joe. Everybody calls me T-Joe." He set down his cup. "I want you to look at a piece of land."

"Where?" I asked, but I already knew.

"A few years ago when oil prices were higher I bought twelve hundred acres in West Feliciana Parish, on the river. Used to be part of Greenbriar Plantation, but the owner was selling it off. It's part pasture, part swamp." He reached under the table and brought out a plastic tube. He extracted a rolled-up map and moved our cups and plates to the adjacent table. Then he spread out the map in front of us. I saw that it was a schematic prepared by a landscape architecture firm in Lafayette.

"My idea was a vacation place for the family," T-Joe explained. "Original landowner kept the plantation house but I took everything up to this fence line." He tapped the center of the map with his pencil. "Here's where I plan to put the house. And we're gonna make a small lake right behind it. There'll be some nature trails, and this part back here, the island, will be left alone, for hunting." I followed his finger across the map to a bulge that extended into the Mississippi.

He folded up the drawing and slipped it back into the tube.

" 'Course, it may all have to wait till oil hits thirty dollars a barrel again."

I didn't tell him he might have a long wait. He seemed like a nice man, the kind who'd made it by hard work and a little luck, and it wasn't for me to pour cold water on his dreams.

"Sounds first-class," I said.

"I think so." He put his hands together, interlocking the fingers, as if he were struggling with what he was about to say. "Alan, I'm from St. Martin Parish. I grew up without anything, and I reckon I've done pretty good for myself. Put myself through LSU in engineering and did a good business selling drilling equipment during the boom days. There were lots of overnight millionaires then, but while they were spending their money, I saved mine. I wanted to have something in a few years, and now I do. So when we bought this land, my wife and me, we got books out of the library and we read everything we could find, about the first explorers, and how LaSalle came down the river with Tonti the Iron Hand and then how, a few years later, in 1699, Iberville and his brother sailed up it. Iberville founded Baton Rouge and his brother founded New Orleans."

I knew the story well. The voyage up the river by Iberville and Bienville had been recorded in Iberville's journal, and it was just as exciting to remember now as the first time I'd read it, years ago.

"They found a lot of Indian tribes. Houma and Bayogoula and Tensa," T-Joe went on. "That's where you come in."

"You want an archaeological survey of your property."

T-Joe leaned over the table until his head was close to mine.

"You know the story of the Tunica tribe?" he asked.

"Reasonably well," I said. "DeSoto found them in northwestern Mississippi in 1541. By the time Iberville came upriver, in 1699, they were in the Yazoo Basin, and by the 1700s they were living in West Feliciana Parish, at what's now Angola Prison."

T-Joe nodded approvingly.

"Right. And by 1731, after a fight with the Natchez, they went a few miles south of Angola, to Trudeau Plantation, and stayed there until 1764. That's where the treasure was found."

"Is your acreage near Trudeau?" I asked, the hairs of my neck prickling.

He ignored the question. "According to Dr. Brain, at Harvard, they left Trudeau because they ambushed some Englishmen and were afraid of revenge. So they ran away to the Gulf Coast and lived in Mobile for about a year, but then they got tired and decided to come home."

"Brain's the world authority," I said, waiting.

"When they came back here, they found a spot about ten miles south of Trudeau and stayed there until 1803, when they moved up the Red River to Marksville. That's where the reservation is today."

He paused for my reaction.

"You've done your homework," I said. "You think you've got a historic Tunica site on your property?"

He nodded. "You remember what Dr. Brain wrote about that last Tunica village, the one they left in 1803?"

"I think he said it was in the river."

"What if I was to tell you Dr. Brain was wrong? What if I was to tell you there was a second Tunica Treasure, as big as the first, and it was somewhere on my land? What if I was to tell you the second Tunica village was twenty miles from Trudeau instead of ten, and that's why nobody found it?"

I was about to change my impression of him as a man with common sense, but before I could answer he was reaching under the table again. This time he came up with a paper bag, from which he removed several objects wrapped in tissue. With a glance around him to ensure that we were still alone, he reverently laid the paper-wrapped objects on the table.

"Go ahead," he said. "Open them up."

The tingling was reaching all the way to my belly now, as I reached with a trembling hand.

When I'd finished unwrapping the little parcels, I knew that T-Joe Dupont was as sane as I was. Because there, in front of me, under the fluorescent lights, were three glass trade beads, a tarnished copper bell, the rusted action of a flintlock pistol, and a marine shell that could only have been part of a necklace.

The last time I'd seen artifacts like these had been at the

museum on the Tunica Reservation where the Tunica Treasure was displayed.

"And that's only part of it," he whispered. "I've got more at the house."

I exhaled, to keep down the butterflies. I'd heard a rumor that the second Tunica village was still out there somewhere, but until now I'd merely shrugged it off as the gossip of locals.

I handed him back the artifacts. "How do you know these are from your land?"

He gave me a faint smile. "I got them from an old black man named Absalom Moon. Absalom's hunted that land for sixty years. When he showed them to me, I asked him to take me to where they came from, but he pretended not to understand. Just said the *woods*. See, Alan, that's the whole problem."

"His memory?"

T-Joe shook his head. "Absalom's got a mind like fly-paper. He can tell you where a certain tree was growing fifty-two years ago, or how big a buck he killed in the winter of '55. He knows every blade of grass on that land, every trail, and how high the water got in '27. He collects arrow points, used to sell them at one of the stores. He knows where to go after it rains to find them. But when it comes to this stuff, his mind suddenly goes blank."

"Interesting," I said. "But it may not be the worst problem. The worst problem is if we find it."

T-Joe made a face. "Yeah, I know. Wife and me talked about it. Poor bastard that found the first Tunica Treasure ended up with everybody mad at him."

"It wasn't because he found the treasure," I reminded him. "It was because he dug on land that wasn't his and destroyed the better part of a hundred Indian graves just to get the burial goods out of the ground."

"Yeah, but you can't tell me the whole tribe wouldn't descend on me if we found something. I heard they've got a new law . . ."

"That's right. You can't disturb an unmarked burial or the burial goods with it without getting a special permit from the state."

"Which nobody is going to issue." He gave a tight smile. "Well, that's okay. You see, Alan, I don't want to disturb it. I just want to know where it is."

He began to rewrap the little objects and replace them in the bag. My eyes lingered on them like I was losing old friends.

"I don't give a damn about treasure. I've got all the money I need. I just think this is *interesting*. If there's something like that on my land, I think it's great. It's something for my kids and their kids to be proud of. I don't aim to tear up anybody's graves, any more than I'd want my family's graves tore up. I just want to know if it's there, and I want to make sure it's preserved. And afterward I don't want every bastard in the state with a metal detector walking all over my lawn. I'd have to hire a private guard force to keep people away."

"I understand. But you have to realize once we determined it was there, we'd be obligated to report it. That's the law. But the records would be confidential, under the State Archaeologist . . ."

"Hell, there's no such thing as confidential when you get the government into the act." He looked forlorn, like I'd snatched away something he loved.

"Of course," I said, "there's another possibility: This may just be an isolated find. Maybe a trail crossed your property. The Tunica were great traders. This may have been a rendezvous point or something."

"I've thought about that," T-Joe said. "But it might not be, either. This land is about twenty river miles south of the first spot, at Trudeau, on the east bank of the river." He sighed. "And the hell of it is, I'll never know unless I get somebody out there to search for it."

"I guess not," I said. "Well, maybe you'd like some time to think about it."

He sighed and nodded, suddenly looking glum.

"Yeah, I guess I do."

We shook hands and I watched him walk away with his treasures. When he was gone I went over to the levee and climbed up the grassy bank to where I could look out at the river. A mile wide here, it had formed both a barrier and a highway in ancient days, connecting tribes as far apart as Louisiana and Illinois. It had seen the Spaniard DeSoto come in 1541, with his rag-tag party of conquistadors, and it had swallowed his body when he'd died of a fever on its banks. It had seen the French explorers after him, and had witnessed the founding of a new country. But most of all, it had seen the first Americans, the Natchez, Bayogoula, Houma, and Tunica. They had depended on it for the fertility of their crops and had traveled on its waters. And through the centuries it had whipsawed its way back and forth across the land like a great snake, wiping out all that had been.

What the hell was I thinking? The second Tunica village was in the river now. Or someone would have found it years ago.

I drove back to our office, an old frame house in Tigertown, just outside the north gates of the university. Not exactly an upscale location, but convenient for research at the library and the university collections. We'd found drunks asleep on our front yard more than once in the ten years we'd been here, but we had a state-of-the-art alarm system, and the location made it easy for us to hire students.

As I walked in Marilyn, my tiny office manager, handed me a message slip.

"Bertha just called, and she sounded hot."

I sighed. Bertha Bomberg, whom we all called Bombast, was our contract officer at the New Orleans District of the Corps of Engineers. A call from her was usually a trial by fire as she inflicted some new theory or demand. I nodded to the pair of students sorting artifacts at the two big tables in what used to be a living room and went straight to my office at the back. Even with the air conditioning the room felt warm, but I knew that when I spoke to Bertha it would get warmer. I leaned back in my chair and propped my feet on the oak desk I'd rescued at a yard sale. I was thinking about T-Joe Dupont and wondering if I ought to get involved. He wanted silence, but there was no way to ensure that. News traveled. So, in all, the work had the potential of getting us some publicity, but I wasn't sure it was the kind of publicity we needed. Contract archaeology isn't like academic archaeology: It's a business where discretion is valued.

I wondered if Bombast would be at her desk now. Today was Friday and she wasn't known for her long hours. Maybe she'd gone home early. Or maybe I could manage to call while she was down the hall at the candy machine, and thus avoid her until Monday. It was eleven o'clock. If she left for lunch at eleven-thirty and didn't return . . .

The phone rang and my spirits sagged.

I lifted the receiver like a man under water and told myself to keep my cool.

"Moundmasters," I said.

"Christ, when are you going to change that goofy name?" a male voice whined. It wasn't Bertha.

"Hello, Freddie," I said. "How did I luck out? First a call from Bombast and now the president of Pyramid Consultants."

"Bombast?" he snorted. "What did you do, fuck up your last delivery order? I told them they should've given us that contract. You can't run a business with part timers and students."

"Is that what you told them when you protested the award?"

"None of your business what we put in our protest. But I didn't call to argue with you. I called because we've got a mutual interest. We need to work together."

"You and me?" My laughter brought Marilyn to poke her head in the doorway. "Freddie, we do *fieldwork* around here. You know, that stuff with shovels and trowels, that gets dirt on you." I had an image of him, across town in his carpeted office, relaxing in his padded executive chair. The last fieldwork he'd been personally involved in was the expansion of the golf course at a country club in Mississippi, and rumor had it he'd supervised his crew from the bar.

"I'll overlook the insult, Al. I know how it is when you get hungry. I'm just trying to make sure neither one of us starves."

"What does that mean?"

"That means there are three contract firms in this parish. Us, you, and CEI. Naturally, we get most of the work, but there've been some crumbs for you and CEI despite your prices. But the fact is we're at about saturation point."

"What do you propose, Don Corleone? We carve up the territory?"

"Very funny, Al. You'll be laughing out of the other side of your mouth if she gets a foothold."

"She *who?*"

"This *woman,* for God's sake! The one who's come down from Yankee land who's setting up a new firm here."

My belly did a little jump. He was right: Competition wasn't welcome in a market that was already on the ropes.

"What are you talking about?" I asked.

"I see I've got your attention. I didn't hear a 'Thank you, Dr. St. Ambrose,' but never mind. I understand."

"Stop babbling, Freddie, and tell me what this is all about."

"I'm *trying* to, Al." His voice rose an octave. "There's a new player in town. She calls herself—now get this— *P. E.* Courtney. She's from Massachusetts, of all places. Got her doctorate from Harvard. Now you tell me what a Harvard Ph.D. is doing down here scraping up jobs in contract archaeology? I'm telling you, Al, something smells."

"It *is* unusual," I agreed.

"Her dissertation was some kind of study of contact sites in the Yazoo Basin. Christ, why doesn't she take a job at some little pissant college in Mississippi?"

"Jobs are hard to get."

"Well, she's going to find that contract archaeology in Louisiana's a hell of a lot tougher. If we stand together on this the jokers at CEI will have to go along . . ."

"Stand together? What do you mean?"

"Freeze her ass out. She came by here to introduce herself and I already told her she wasn't welcome. I assume I spoke for you, too."

"Wait a minute . . ."

"Listen, Al." His voice had that low, earnest tone that meant somebody was about to get screwed. "If we make it hot enough for her, she'll go away. I know what women are like. I've been married three times. We can freeze her ass out with low bids, just you and me. CEI can't touch us—their overhead's too high. But I'll let a couple of people go if I have to, take a temporary loss. If you'll do the same . . ."

"I think that's illegal," I said.

"It's *business*, for Christ's sake."

"Not my kind."

"Al, you're a born sucker."

"And you were born to be hanged." I slammed the receiver down, which was par for the course after talking with Freddie St. Ambrose for more than two minutes. Still, this wasn't good news. We existed on the thin line between survival and bankruptcy as it was. Another player could tip any of us right over.

P. E. Courtney.

I ate a bag lunch at the sorting table with Marilyn and Gator, our gap-toothed field boss, so named for his tendency to abandon survey to wrestle alligators when he saw one basking. A good man, and so far indestructible. I was wadding up my lunch papers when David Goldman returned from the library. An ex-rabbinical student from New Orleans, David had surprised his family by dropping his theological studies to take up anthropology. He'd come to Louisiana State for a master's and had joined me the year before his graduation, first as a part-timer and then as a full-time archaeologist. His specialty was lithics, and he'd written several papers on the sources of the stone used in some of the tools found at the great Poverty Point site in the northeastern part of the state. I told him about my meeting with T-Joe and he shrugged.

"Probably nothing to it," he said. "He could've gotten the damn things anywhere. I've seen them being sold in curio stores in the French Quarter, in New Orleans."

I nodded reluctantly. "I don't think he's the kind that would fall for a hoax," I said. "And he seemed honest himself."

"Maybe," David said and headed for his own office, a remodeled bedroom next to my own lair. I started to mention my conversation with Freddie, but it seemed unnecessary.

I read through the printout of the *Commerce and Business Daily*, looking for bid solicitations on newly announced government projects. I found nothing but a request for a cultural resources survey in Hawaii, and turned to the draft of a report we'd done for a construction company on a pipeline right-of-way. I was midway through the boilerplate chapter on prehistory when I heard voices in the lab. A few seconds later a frowning Marilyn appeared in my doorway.

"Alan, there's somebody to see you."

"Oh?" I wondered for a minute if Freddie had decided to come in person to press his point, but decided it was unlikely: It took a lot to budge Freddie St. Ambrose from his padded chair. Probably a student looking for a part-time job for the rest of the summer.

"Show him in," I said.

"*Her*," Marilyn said primly. "Your him's a her."

"Oh. And does *her* have a name?" I asked.

Marilyn, ever jealous of her position as factotum, nodded.

"She *says* her name is P. E. Courtney."

▰▰TWO

I rose slowly, but before I could get around my desk she was inside.

"You're Alan Graham," she said.

I nodded, not yet sure what to say. The woman in front of me wore a Liz Claiborne suit and carried a slim, executive attaché case. Her blond hair was clipped short, and designer glasses magnified frank brown eyes. There was a woman under there someplace, I decided, an attractive woman, but I wasn't sure she knew it after all the power statements.

"And you're . . ."

"P. E. Courtney. Here's my card."

She thrust out a square of cardboard and I read what it said:

COURTNEY & ASSOCIATES
Cultural Resource Consultants
6006 Perkins Road, Suite 107
Baton Rouge, LA 70808

(504) 555-ARCH

P. E. Courtney, Ph.D.
President

I wondered who the "associates" were, but, then, everybody had associates, even if they were the night cleaning crew.

"What can I do for you?" I asked, shaking her hand. Her grip was firm, and I noticed she had the thin fingers of a pianist. No rings. On either hand.

"May I sit down?"

I went to pull over a chair but she already had it.

"Thanks." She sat and I dropped back into my own chair, wondering if I'd misjudged Freddie.

"You're probably asking yourself why I'm here. The reason's simple: I wanted to introduce myself before rumors started to circulate. So I'm making the rounds of the local contract firms." She dug into her attaché case and came up with a brochure.

"This is a prospectus for our company. I'd like you to have it."

It was printed on slick paper, in six colors. It said Courtney & Associates could do just about anything. Some of the associates were listed. They were big names in the Eastern archaeology establishment, but I'd never known any to stoop from their academic chairs long enough to get involved in contract work.

"Impressive," I said. "But I think I'd ask myself how much the economy will support down here."

"Just so it supports one more," she said, showing me her teeth. "You see, Alan—may I call you Alan?—"

I nodded.

"Good. And I'm P. E." She looped an arm over the back of her chair. "I'm here because I want to be. I got my degree from Harvard last year, and all my professors thought I was going to shoot for a university position. But I inherited some money from an aunt and I wanted to work in Louisiana. I like it here." Another barracuda smile. "I'm here to stay."

"You're from back East," I commented.

"Massachusetts. But I've always liked the South, ever since I was young and traveled down here. I did an analysis last year and decided that, while the Louisiana economy is questionable just now, it has more potential than any other state in the region."

"Well, all I can say is good luck."

"Thanks. But I don't think I'll need luck. I'm good enough to succeed without it."

"Oh?" My jaw clenched. I was starting to feel positively sympathetic toward Freddie.

"I'm not bragging," she said. "It's an objective statement. I realize self-confidence offends some people."

"Imagine."

She nodded. "I was talking to Fred St. Ambrose earlier today. I don't think he understood."

I suppressed a smile. "Oh? What did he tell you?"

"Well, *first* he tried to hire me. He said some oil man was trying to have some work done on his property and it might involve colonial period Tunica artifacts."

I flinched.

"What did you say?"

"I said I thought it would be interesting and I offered to subcontract the lab work."

"What then?"

She shrugged. "Nothing. He started talking about how the Indians were ruining things for archaeology and he wanted to know how discreet I was, and I had a funny feeling he wanted me to help him get around the unmarked burials law."

"And?"

"I turned him down. That was when he got really insulting. Said I'd never work in Louisiana, he had the contracts *and* the contacts. He claimed I'd, quote, sink up to your little ass in debt, unquote, which I guess I ought to take as a compliment. The bit about the little ass, I mean."

"What did you do?"

"I walked. The man's a sleaze. Are all the contract archaeologists in the state like him?"

"You'll have to make up your own mind about that," I said dryly. "Freddie comes from an old New Orleans family. Trouble is it was originally *Ambrosio,* in the Ninth Ward. He got a degree in business and an anthropology minor, and then, back when contract archaeology started heating up in the late seventies, he took an M.A. here at LSU. Then he got some kind of life experience doctorate from an alternative university that doesn't make you go to classes or take tests, so he could call himself *doctor.*"

"They allow that here?" Her brows rose in amazement.

"In the old days they allowed almost anything. Besides, all it takes is an M.A., and his is legitimate enough."

"Amazing," she said. "But *your* doctorate is legitimate, isn't it?"

"If the University of Arizona's still in business."

The penciled brows rose a fraction more. "Not a bad school. Top twenty."

"Something like that," I mumbled, growing more irritated with every second. She brought her arm down and folded her hands on her lap.

"So are *you* going to do the Tunica work?" she asked suddenly. "Because if you are, we'd like to do the artifact analyses."

I stared at her. "What makes you think I'm going to be involved?"

"St. Ambrose sounded pretty desperate for somebody to do the lab work. My guess is that without an expert he may not be able to pull it off. So if you're going to bid, I'd like to work with you. I'll work up a cost proposal, of course. I'm not cheap, but I do good work."

"And the unmarked graves law?"

"I suspect you aren't the kind to break any laws. If it turns out the artifacts are associated with burials, you'll report it."

I nodded. "If something develops, I'll let you know."

She stared me in the eyes. "You know, I could make a bid of my own, without either one of you. And I just might underbid you both."

"You could if you knew who it was that wanted the work done. If you could convince this person somebody from back East knows more about this sort of thing than somebody who's been doing archaeology here for almost ten years."

"Jeff Brain is from back East," she said, and could tell she'd scored. Jeffrey P. Brain was the world's authority on the Tunica Treasure and was, until recently, at Harvard.

"Are you going to subcontract Brain?" I asked.

"I may." She gave me a pussycat smile and I saw she had dimples. She must have seen me staring because her mouth straightened out suddenly.

"Well, you've got to do what you think's best," I said. She got up and extended a hand.

"It's been great meeting you, Alan. I hope we run into each other again soon."

I wasn't sure I shared her hope, and her composure aggravated me. Did she really think she was going to walk in off the street and start taking our business? I skimmed over the brochure again and then thrust it far back into my desk drawer with last year's bid notice from the Forest Service.

My mood only worsened as the afternoon wore on. It reached bottom when I fielded a call from one of our clients, a man named Hayes, whose firm was one link in an involved chain of subcontractors in a retirement village development. He wanted to know when our report would be ready and he didn't want to hear about how many artifacts we'd had to analyze and illustrate.

When I asked him about the 50 percent payment we'd been due for two months, his tone changed to a whine. The prime contractor hadn't paid his company and how could we expect . . . ?

I told him we did expect and that we'd send the report when we saw a check.

He mumbled something about blackmail and said he'd see what he could do. I hung up the phone and watched Marilyn creep through the door with her printout.

"No check from Diversified Consultants?" she asked.

"He said he'd look into it."

"We don't have enough right now to meet payroll next Friday." She started to put the papers in front of me but I waved them away.

"I believe you. I'm still hoping they'll come through. If not, maybe Clarence at the bank will give me a home equity loan."

She nodded and faded back out. Four-thirty came none too soon.

I drove home to my house in the Garden District, thinking of T-Joe Dupont. I didn't know how much he had in mind for a survey, but anything would come in handy right now.

The old house greeted me with creaks as I moved across the front porch. It was a Victorian structure of two stories with bow windows, built in the early days of the century when this was the suburbs. My parents had purchased it in the forties and it was the place I remembered as home. I'd gone away and studied archaeology and then landed a position at a good university. But on a dig in Mexico I'd met a woman, a Mexican archaeologist named Felicia, and I'd loved her too much for my own good. My work had gone to hell, my job had collapsed around me, and one day I'd come back here and started again. I still kept the old furniture and paintings, but I'd put in a dishwasher and central air. And a burglar alarm, because the city had long since moved past Park Boulevard, the main avenue of the district, leaving it perched precariously on the edge of a ghetto. I heated up a couple of frozen meat pies, fed Digger, my Shepherd mixed breed, and turned on a ball game. Before the third inning I found myself thinking of P. E. Courtney again.

Brusque, that's what she was. And opinionated. But, then, my father had always said that was the way Yankees were. So maybe she couldn't help it. But *P. E.*? Surely the damn girl had a name. What was it? Patricia? How about Penelope? No, Prudence. I grinned to myself. Yes, that was probably it. *Prudence Elvira.* I liked it.

The next day, Saturday, I jogged around the lakes and did some painting on my garage. I'd been working on it off and on all spring. At this rate, I'd be finished by winter. Maybe. I slapped on the paint in the form of a question mark and then brushed it over. All I needed was a nosy Yankee woman. And a good-looking one, at that. The prospect nagged me all through that night's poker game, and a couple of the players commented that my usually famous jambalaya was overcooked.

On Sunday I slept until ten, made myself bacon and eggs for brunch, took Digger for a flea dip at the vet school, and then for a drying-out run atop the levee.

Absalom Moon. Who the hell knew where he'd gotten those artifacts? It could be like chasing a will-o'-the-wisp. Worse, it could turn into a no-win situation, and I was always careful to turn down those kinds of projects. Still, it could save our payroll, and if it worked out, we could make a major discovery, and there weren't many of those.

By the time I got home that afternoon I decided I'd take the job. As for the payroll, I'd go down to the bank tomorrow and talk to Clarence about a second mortgage on my house. Maybe if I threw myself on the floor and begged he'd extend us another few thousand. What good would it do his bank if we went belly-up owing them money?

I'd just finished my shower and was drying off when the phone rang. I swore under my breath and stumbled down the hallway to the phone.

I jerked it to my ear. "Hello?"

"Dr. Graham?" The voice was vaguely familiar.

"Yes?"

"This is Willie Dupont, T-Joe's son. You talked to my dad Friday, about some work up near Greenbriar."

There was something oddly somber about his tone.

"I remember."

There was a long silence and then he said: "My dad's dead."

It took a moment for the news to sink in.

"What?"

"Yeah. He went out yesterday to talk to Carter Wascom, the man he bought the land from. When he left, his car ran off the road not a half-mile from our place. He hit a tree and it broke his neck."

"I'm sorry," I said. The words sounded pitifully inadequate. I'd liked T-Joe. And, insensitive as it seemed, there *was* the payroll to think about.

"I'd like to go to the funeral," I said.

"No." His determination took me by surprise. "The funeral's Tuesday, in Breaux Bridge. You can't do any good there. Your place is doing what my dad was hiring you to do.''

Had I heard him right?

"You mean . . . ?''

"I talked to Mama and my sister Dominique. This land meant a lot to Dad. It's why he got killed, in a way. I mean, if he hadn't bought the land, he wouldn't have been on that road, would he? So we want to go ahead with it. We want to make the land the way he wanted it, just like he was here. Once a Dupont decides on something, ain't nobody keeps it from happening.''

There wasn't anything for me to say.

▰▰▰THREE

Willie Dupont came in the next morning. He looked the way I figured his dad must've looked in his mid-twenties: stocky and muscular, with dark wavy hair and a square jaw. Despite his red eyes, his grief seemed to have been replaced by determination, as if he could will the death of his father away by becoming the agent of T-Joe's dream. He was, however, thoroughly familiar with the project, having been involved at every step.

We laid Willie's map out on one of the lab tables, and David and I examined the terrain. It was rough, with steep, forested hills that fell away sharply to a floodplain about a half-mile wide. A finger formed by a dried-up bayou had cut a section of the floodplain away from the rest of the land, so that it became an island, though the only real water was that of the river, on its west side.

"I'll need some time to put together a budget," I said, but Willie shook his head.

"Tell me how much you need to start and you can figure out the budget later."

David and I exchanged glances. It would take a team of four to five archaeologists, armed with metal detectors, probes, and shovels, and we might want to do a more formal search with a magnetometer. Not to mention the archival research I'd throw in the lap of our historian, Esmerelda.

"It won't be cheap," I hedged.

"I don't expect it to be. But my dad trusted you and I do, too."

David said, "We can't promise success. All we can do is use the best methodology we have. The site could be there and we might still miss it. Or it might not even be there at all."

"Look, I've been around the oil business since I was a kid. Odds of hitting on an exploration well are about one in seven, and even a shallow well costs you thirty grand. Well, it's our land and our money. Now, how much do you need to start today?"

I calculated mentally. "Eight thousand to start," I said. "If we have to go the whole route with magnetometry, it'll probably cost another eight or nine. If we luck out and locate something with shovel testing, the whole job shouldn't go over ten or twelve."

Willie pulled out a checkbook.

"I'll pay you eight now," he said. "I have my mother's power of attorney. You can call the bank if you want."

"Don't you want to draw something up?"

"My dad worked on handshakes all his life," he said. "I don't plan to change things now."

I hesitated, exchanged glances again with David, and then shrugged.

"Done," I said, giving him my hand. "We'll get started today."

Willie wrote out a check, tore it out of his checkbook, and handed it to me. It had barely touched my fingers before Marilyn had whisked it away.

"This is all new to me," he said. "Before this, I'd've thought the best place to find an archaeologist was in the university."

"Used to be," I told him. "But that was the old days. The environmental laws of the sixties and seventies created contract archaeology. It's as much a business as a scientific discipline."

"Of course, the academic archaeologists look down on us," David put in. "It's easy with a guaranteed salary and all the time in the world to do your work. But the funny thing is there are more of us than there are of them."

"That's America," Willie said. He looked idly over at the bookshelf and lifted down a copy of Bass's *Human Osteology.* "You fool with human bones much?"

"Not anymore," I said. "These days it's mostly animals."

He grunted. "How many teeth a human being have?"

David and I looked at each other.

"Thirty-two," we said together.

Willie nodded glumly. "Never saw one with thirty-three?"

I shook my head. "No. Why?"

"My dad had thirty-three," Willie said. "What do you think of that?"

"Thirty-three teeth?" David asked. "You mean a mutation?"

"I don't know what I mean. All I know is when he hit the steering wheel a couple of his front teeth and an eyetooth got knocked out. They picked 'em up from the floor of the car. And a bicuspid, too."

"A bicuspid?" I said, not sure where he was going. "But that's in the side of the mouth. A frontal blow . . ."

"You don't understand," Willie said and turned to face me, pain showing in his face. "He had all his teeth: There wasn't any bicuspid missing."

"That's impossible," David said.

"Tell me about it," Willie said. "But there it was, big as hell, filling and all. Coroner showed it to me. That's why I'm having my own autopsy done. Rest of the family's mad as hell. They want me to leave him in peace. But I want to know if this guy screwed up my father's autopsy. Isn't anything wrong with wanting to know how your father died, is there?"

I shook my head. "No."

"I mean, maybe it wasn't an accident. I know Carter Wascom's got second thoughts about selling him the land. That's why Dad went to talk to him. Or maybe there's something about that treasure somebody doesn't want to be found."

"You think Wascom could have murdered your father?" I asked.

"I don't know. But I'm damn sure gonna find out."

I took a deep breath.

"Willie, are you hiring us to do a survey or find the truth about your father's death?"

Willie gave a lopsided smile. "Way I figure, Dr. Graham, you do one and you may end up doing the other. You ready to go?"

"Now?"

"Sure," Willie said. "I can drive you up and show you where it happened and then I'll take you around to see old Absalom."

"The man who found the artifacts?"

"That's him. He's a slippery old rascal, but he keeps his eyes open. He won't talk to a cop but maybe he'll talk to an archaeologist."

"All right," I said, turning around to get my notebook and a topographic map.

Absalom wasn't the only slippery person in this business, I thought, as we walked out to Willie's Bronco. T-Joe's son was a pretty slick character himself.

St. Francisville, half an hour north of Baton Rouge, perches on the bluffs overlooking the Mississippi. The first settlement, Bayou Sara, was long ago claimed by the river. The present town has a Gothic courthouse, an antebellum Episcopal cemetery, and several antique shops. The people are largely from English and Scottish stock, unlike the Cajuns spread out along the floodplain to the south.

There's also a nuclear reactor, about five miles south of the town itself. It was built in the seventies, when nuclear energy sounded like a good idea. The company's customers have been paying for it ever since. Sensitive to the term *nuclear*, the utility company has posted signs describing it as an *energy center*, as if omitting the offensive word could change popular opinion or make utility rates go down.

It was just south of the reactor plant that we turned, heading left, toward the river, in the shade of moss-bearded oaks and pecans. Willie tensed as we left the highway, and I knew he was thinking about returning to where his father had died.

"We went horseback riding up here last Saturday," he said. "Me, my mom and dad, my sisters, and some of our cousins. Then we had a *cochon d'lait*." He exhaled, his eyes straight ahead. "My Dad was a good driver. No alcohol in his body. They said he wasn't going more than fifty, but he hit the wheel hard enough to bust up his mouth."

He pulled to the side of the road and pointed to a telephone pole on the opposite side. The pole was new, but there was a scatter of glass on the roadway next to it.

"He snapped the pole when he hit it," Willie explained. "They put up a new one right afterward. I prowled around in the ditch when they were finished but I didn't find anything."

I was staring at the roadway.

"You see it, too, then," Willie said.

"What's that?" I asked

"Nothing." He pointed down at the dark asphalt. "That's the problem, see what I mean?"

I heard David's breath suck in, and I knew he was starting to doubt Willie's sanity.

Then I understood what Willie was talking about.

"There aren't any skid marks," I said.

"Right." Willie nodded with a grim smile. "He just plowed right into it like it wasn't even there."

He put the Bronco into gear and pulled back onto the roadway.

"Why did the owner of Greenbriar sell your family the land?" David asked then. "Is the plantation on hard times?"

"Sort of." He slowed as we entered a turn. "Carter Wascom's wife died a couple of years back. He blames the nuclear plant. Some kind of cancer he thinks came from dumping wastes. He hired all kinds of lawyers and private detectives but all they did was bleed him dry. The thing got thrown out of court and he ended up having to pay the expert witnesses and court costs. Then I hear the company sued him for defamation and got a judgment.

"Our land's just the other side of that fence." Willie pointed. "I think we got the best acreage. He didn't really want to let us have it all, but we made him a good offer."

"But you said he was having second thoughts," I said.

"My dad got a call from him right before he went up here. Carter wanted to talk to him, he said. He didn't tell what it was about, just that he was being a pain in the ass."

We slowed at another gate. This one was open. Through the fence I saw a pasture, with a tree line a few hundred yards back.

"Our land goes all the way to the river," Willie said.

The pasture ended with a fence line and on the other side of the fence was a big white house with columns, set back from the road, with a gazebo to one side and a lane of pecan trees leading to the front door. A sign on the front gate said GREENBRIAR. The gate was closed. Just the other side of the plantation was a low, white frame house with a screen porch, with a pickup truck out front, and a satellite dish in the yard. Probably the overseer's place, I thought.

A second house was just beyond this one, and it was there that we stopped. Little more than a shack, the structure was raised above the dirt on cast cement blocks. Chickens pecked in the yard, and a scrawny dog hoisted itself from beside the gate as we turned in. There was a little vegetable garden with a scarecrow off to the side.

"Absalom's place," Willie said.

As I opened my door an old man appeared on the front porch. Lanky, with red suspenders striping a checkered shirt, he had skin the color of coal. Deep-set, lively eyes considered us under a head of short, grizzled gray hair.

"Morning, Absalom," Willie greeted. "I brought a couple of fellows to talk to you about history."

Absalom Moon gave a little nod, his hands thrust deep into his pockets.

"Bad 'bout your dad," he said.

"Yeah," Willie agreed.

Willie told him our names and the old man nodded again. "Well, come up on the porch," he said in a high-pitched voice. "No good standing out in the sun."

We trooped up the rickety wooden steps and Absalom pointed to a couple of aluminum lawn chairs with plastic webbing that was about to fall through. He took a seat in a wooden swing, unconcerned about the fact that one of us would have to stand.

"David, huh?" he said in a half-amused tone, then looked over at my companion: "You don't look like my daddy."

Willie frowned but David, standing behind me, smiled at the biblical allusion: "And you don't look like my son. If I had one . . ."

Absalom chuckled with delight. "Bet you ain't got no boy named Amon, neither."

"No, but my father's name is Solomon," David told him. "Only people call him Sol."

"I be jiggered," Absalom said. "You not from 'round here, though."

"New Orleans."

"I be jiggered."

Willie leaned forward: "I told them about the Indian things you found."

I felt Absalom withdraw and wished Willie had kept quiet.

"Lots of Indian things," Absalom said vaguely, sitting back against the swing. "Arrowheads, mostly. Wash out after it rain."

"I'm talking about the beads," Willie said. "And the copper bells."

Absalom's eyes dropped away. "Arrowheads what most folks want," he commented. "I got some big as your hand."

"Did you find the other stuff with the arrowheads, then?" Willie asked.

"Arrowheads mostly alone," the old man said. He looked over at David and me. "You hunt arrowheads?"

We both nodded. "Whenever we can find them," David told him.

"Look, Absalom," Willie broke in. "I'll pay you to show me where that other stuff came from."

Absalom shook his head sadly. "Mr. Willie, I wants to help you, but I just plain have trouble remembering. Now them arrowheads . . ."

Willie got up from the chair. "At least tell me if the stuff came from our land."

"Well, I think they comes from your land. But you know how it is, Mr. Willie. That river change everything. Back there in the woods there ain't no fences. I probably couldn't find the place again nohow."

Willie shrugged. "Fair enough. By the way, were you here when my father came up to see Mr. Wascom the other day?"

Absalom looked away quickly. "Bad thing, 'bout Mr. Joe," he said. "I didn't see nothin', though. Wasn't here."

There was no mistaking his fear.

Willie started down the steps, fanning himself with his baseball cap. "Okay, Absalom. We won't bother you anymore."

"Ain't no bother, suh."

I waited for David to step down ahead of me and then turned to the old man.

"Were there bones with these Indian things, by any chance?"

His eyes met mine and then fell away quickly.

"Can't say I wants to fool with no bones," he said in a low voice.

I understood then and nodded in agreement. We were out of the driveway and back on the tartop before Willie spoke.

"See what I mean? He knows exactly where those things come from. And I'll bet he saw Dad stop at Wascom's place." He slowed as he passed the plantation house, then muttered under his breath. There was no car in the drive, and I had a feeling he'd meant to call on Carter Wascom, with us for witnesses.

Then his foot hit the brake and the Bronco slowed. We were passing his land now and he was looking through the fence at a blue pickup that hadn't been in the field when we passed the first time.

"That's strange," he muttered and turned into the field through the open gate. "I wonder who's back there."

We bumped along through the grass and jerked to a stop behind the truck. Willie's door flew open and David and I got out behind him. The June sun hit me like a blast from a furnace.

Willie reached under the seat and withdrew a long-barreled revolver, which he stuck down into his belt.

"Can't be too careful," he said. "But it's probably just somebody picking dewberries."

Even as his door shut two men emerged from the trees on the far side of the pasture, a black Labrador gamboling through the grass beside them.

"It's Carter Wascom," he said.

We followed as he walked toward the pair. As we got closer, I saw that one man was tall, with gray hair and a slight limp, while the other was on the chunky side and balding. The tall man wore jeans and an open-necked blue shirt and carried a short-barreled carbine in one hand, while the other man was dressed in khakis.

"Something the matter, Mr. Wascom?" Willie asked.

Carter Wascom offered Willie a hand and Willie introduced each of us. Wascom's hand felt soft as silk, and when he spoke his lips barely moved. "It was terrible about your father. I can't tell you how sorry I am. I found him, you know."

Willie nodded.

"He came up here to see you, didn't he?" Willie asked.

"Why, yes. We were talking about another little piece of land your father wanted and I wasn't sure I wanted to sell." He chuckled.

"What was the outcome?"

"I told him I'd think about it. Then he went down the road to see old Absalom. An hour later I saw his car go by and then I heard the crash."

"Your truck?" Willie asked.

Carter Wascom jerked his head toward his companion. "It's Levi's. I was taking him back to the bayou." He lifted his rifle. "That's why I have this. A .22 magnum makes a good argument with snakes."

The short man stuck out his hand then.

"I'm Levi Goodeau." He had a round, good-natured face, a contrast to the ascetic, almost suffering countenance of his companion. "I hope we weren't trespassing. I'd hate to run up against that Smith." He nodded at the revolver in Willie's belt.

"No problem," Willie said. "Only person has to worry about this is the one that killed my father."

"Killed?" Wascom asked. "You don't think it was accidental?"

"No."

"Dear me. Well, don't do anything rash. You don't want to end up as Levi's guest."

And I remembered where I'd heard Goodeau's name.

"You're the warden at Angola," I said.

Levi Goodeau shrugged. "That's me. I took a few hours off to come down and see Carter. We're cousins, you know."

Carter Wascom nodded. "I was going to show him what's flowing in the bayou. I was trying to prove I'm not the only one that's affected."

"What are you talking about?" Willie asked.

"Come on back. I'll show you," Wascom said and we followed him out of the pasture and into the woods, the dog bounding along beside us.

The sun's glare abated, but the humidity was high, so that rivers of sweat were streaming down my arms and I felt my shirt sticking to my back. The ground smelled of decayed vegetation and my feet sank into the soft leaves. Out of habit, I kept my eyes down, looking for snakes.

We were on a finger ridge, an ancient plateau of finely ground clay that jutted out into the floodplain of a small bayou which, in its turn, joined the Mississippi River a mile or so to the west. When we threaded our way through the last red oaks and stood on the edge of the bluff, Carter Wascom pointed at the area below.

"Can't see it from here, but down there's the bayou. You game to go look?"

"Why not?" Willie asked and we followed down the bank, grabbing at vines and tree roots as we went. The bottom, twenty feet below the bluff, was sand, deposited from endless cycles of flooding. Wascom was already at the water's edge, pointing, and when I came even with him I saw what he was talking about. There was a sudsy-looking residue on top of the water, floating gently toward the river.

"This bayou goes right past that damn nuclear plant," he accused. "You can't tell me they aren't dumping something into it."

I stared down at the suds. Wherever it was coming from, it was a stain on what would otherwise have been a primeval setting.

"It couldn't have come from some other place, say another house, or maybe a dump?" I asked.

Carter Wascom withered me with his stare.

"My wife died, sir, and it wasn't from *some other place* or *house* or *dump*. She was a beautiful woman and she died a cruel, agonizing death. Cancer of the liver. It spread." He took a deep breath and went on: "For several years, before the disease was diagnosed, there was this scum on the surface of the bayou. Only none of us knew what it was then. It was the first year that abomination they call a nuclear plant was in operation. After I raised enough hell with them, the stuff stopped for a while. Now ..." He pointed down like an Old Testament prophet. "It's started again." He turned on Willie. "That's what I told your father, that anything he bought now was ruined anyway, I didn't want to take his money that way."

I saw Willie shoot a questioning look at Levi Goodeau. The warden put a hand on his cousin's shoulder. "Well, Carter, I think you're right to have some samples taken. Maybe that'll get to the bottom once and for all."

Wascom gave his kinsman a skeptical look. "Like it did before? They ruined the samples at the lab. Those people got to them, had them say the samples were *innocuous, if you can believe that*. Levi, you're too decent a man for your job. How can you run a farm full of cutthroats when you can't even see how deeply the corruption has reached into every part of this state?"

"Oh, Carter, it's not that bad," Goodeau said. "Come on. Let's get back and have some lemonade."

I thought Wascom was going to argue, but suddenly the fight seemed to have gone out of him. His shoulders slumped and I saw confusion in his face.

"Lemonade," he said. "Yes, I suppose we ought to.

I . . ." He looked from one of us to the other. "I'm sorry if I involved you in my private problems. I just think . . ." He raised his hands in supplication. "This has to be everybody's problem. Doesn't it?"

"Of course, Carter." Goodeau helped his cousin to the base of the bluff and waited patiently while the tall man scrambled to the top. When Wascom was halfway up, the warden turned to us and shrugged apologetically.

He needn't have, though. I'd seen the suds, and wherever they were from, they'd ruined the bayou.

≡ FOUR

It was early afternoon when we got back to the office. There were three message slips from Bertha Bomberg on my desk. The first one said *Urgent*, the second said *Extremely urgent*, and the third said *Call before two!!!* It was now one-fifty-six. With a sigh, I dialed her number at the Corps of Engineers and hoped that she'd still be out to lunch and the call would switch over to one of her less obnoxious office mates.

But when I heard the line click on the second ring I knew there would be no further reprieves.

"Bomberg, Planning."

"Hi, Bertha, this is Alan." I tried to put some cheer in my voice. "Looks like we've been missing each other."

"Have you been avoiding me, Alan?"

"Not at all. I tried you Friday and I was out all this morning."

"I was sick Friday. I went home early. I'm *still* sick. I shouldn't even be in the office at all."

"I'm sorry." I tried to sound as if I really was.

"Thank you. Alan, I have some questions about the report you did for us on the Plaquemine Revetment."

"The one we did three years ago."

"Is that a criticism?"

"Not at all."

"Good. Because I *am* the government."

A bad sign, I thought: She usually saved that part for last and now she was sticking it in at the beginning.

"Is there a problem with the report, Bertha?"

"If there wasn't, would I be calling?"

I made an indecipherable sound.

I heard papers rustling on her desk.

"Now," she said. "I have a lot of corrections, and I'm going to send them all to you, with the marked draft copy, but there was one, I guess I should say, glaring problem."

I entertained a vision of having to send a crew back into the field and taking a ten-thousand-dollar loss.

"A problem?" I swallowed.

"Yes. I'm surprised you didn't find it yourself. You *do* read over these things, don't you?"

"Of course."

"Well, then, why didn't anybody catch the problem of the levee?"

"The levee?" A cold shudder ran through me. Had one of our maps put it in the wrong place?

"The levee," she repeated. "You didn't look under it."

"Under it? Fifty tons of dirt?"

"Your history section clearly states that the levee wasn't built until the 1920s. That was thirty years after Darling Plantation was divided up after a sheriff's sale."

"So?"

Her voice took on an air of impatience as she instructed her wayward child:

"So there may be cultural resources under the present levee. Did you look for them?"

Silence as I visualized the levee, a thirty-foot-tall pile of dirt.

"How do you look under a levee?" I said.

"That's not the point," she shot back.

"I don't understand."

"Evidently. And that's why we may have to have a meeting."

"A meeting?"

"To address this kind of inadequacy. You'll get the report by FedEx tomorrow. I expect to hear from you as soon as you've read the comments." There was an audible sigh. "Alan, I can promise you, when the next contracts are bid, this issue will come up."

"So what do you want us to do?"

"You'll have my comments in writing. I see no purpose in talking on the phone about it. That only leads to misunderstandings."

"Goodbye, Bertha."

"Goodbye." The line went dead and I replaced the receiver.

David appeared in the doorway. "So what was all that about?"

"Looking under levees," I said.

"Oh," he said. "The same-old, same-old."

I got up from my desk and made two fists. "Someday that goddamn woman . . ."

"Now you know why they had the flood of '27," he said. I didn't think Bombast was that old, but I wasn't going to dispute it.

Understand: I am not against women. I find them wonderful and intriguing creatures, and once I even married one. But there are times when it seems that I, a poor male, am beset by the worst the other sex has to offer. First P. E. Courtney, offering to take away my business, and now Bombast, the corps battle-ax, feeding her neuroses.

Give me two miles of briars to walk through any day.

I picked up my morning paper, telling myself that gnashing my teeth accomplished nothing. If I looked through the news I'd find people with far worse trials to endure than a gauntlet of harpies. Not that Courtney was a harpy, exactly. Stripped of the power clothing, she might look pretty good. Stripped . . .

CONTRACTOR ACCUSED OF CHEATING GOVERNMENT.

I sighed as my eye picked out the headline. I already felt sorry for the poor bastard. Why didn't headlines ever say DRONES CHEAT GOVERNMENT, and detail the endless meetings, coffee breaks, and training sessions that gobbled the taxpayers' money? But no, it was always some poor devil trying to keep his company's head above water.

Okay, so I'm biased.

Then my eye fell on a headline in the "People" section: ANGOLA WARDEN BELIEVES IN REHABILITATION.

And there was a photo of a smiling Levi Goodeau. I

skimmed the story, picking out the facts that Goodeau had a doctorate in sociology and was the first warden of the penitentiary ever to hold such a credential. He'd worked his way up, serving as a counselor and an assistant warden, while attending graduate school at night, and all along he'd retained his faith in humankind. I wondered how that was possible, but graduate school has a way of warping people. He'd held his post for only a few months and he'd made a number of substantial changes: increasing educational opportunities and hiring more counselors. I sympathized with the sentiments, but I hoped he wasn't a fool; the warden's job was no place for somebody with a weak stomach. Three thousand hardcore convicts could shake Mother Teresa's faith in humanity.

I was folding the newspaper when David walked in.

"I finished the Allison report," he said. "So I've got some time."

"Time for what?" I asked.

He grinned in his little-boy way.

"Well, I thought maybe if I went back and talked to old Absalom, I might get a little more out of him. He seemed to be interested in the fact that we were connected by our first names. If he's a Bible reader, I figure I can hold my own."

It was my turn to smile: David was a Talmudic scholar and could hold his own in a room full of Jesuits. More importantly, though, he had a way of talking to people, and I'd seen him succeed in gaining rapport more than once where others, including me, had failed.

"Take the cell phone," I said.

"Keep it," he replied. "I'm just going up for a couple of hours."

I shrugged. "Then call me tonight. If we have to put a team into the field, we're going to have to call some folks in a hurry."

I watched him leave, wishing I could go, too. But being away all morning had left me with a stack of paperwork and some letters to write. My progress, however, was desultory. I couldn't stop thinking of T-Joe, dead at the wheel of a car that had left no skid marks. A dead man with more

teeth than nature allows. Finally, I succumbed and called
the forensics anthropology lab at the university. I was in
luck: The phone was picked up by the lab head herself, an
intense young woman named Chloe Messner. She pronounced on the skeletons that turned up in weed-grown lots
and sorted out the victims of plant explosions. She loved
the outré, so I didn't waste time:

"Ever worked with the coroner of West Feliciana?"

"Once or twice. Why, Alan? You have something for
me?"

"Sorry, not quite."

"Oh." The disappointment was clear in her tone.

"I was just curious about what kind of job they do up
there."

"Depends. I think they send most of their clients to
Baton Rouge. Better facilities."

It conjured the image of a hotel with a spa for the dead
and hot and cold running formaldehyde, and I shuddered.

"So the pathologist here would find out if an accident
wasn't an accident."

"Theoretically. But it isn't always easy to tell. I saw a
hit-and-run victim once, beautiful girl, from her picture;
she'd been lying in a field for a month and the insects had
done their work, so—"

"I get the idea," I said, cutting her off before I gagged.
"And he'd figure out if a body had too many teeth."

"Come again?"

"If the victim had thirty-three teeth instead of your
government-issue thirty-two."

"Alan, do you know somebody like that?" The
excitement was back in her voice and I knew she was visualizing a research publication.

"I don't know. I just know of a case where the victim
in a car accident had some teeth knocked out and when
they scooped them up from the floor of the car he had an
extra premolar, filling and all."

"That's impossible. There must've been somebody else
in the car."

"Who got their tooth knocked out and then ran away?"

"Stranger things have happened. I remember the case of

a woman they found burned up in her bedroom and there was a wooden leg in the bathtub. They went back through the rubble a second time looking for another body. Turned out she was killed by her husband, who set the house on fire while she was with her one-legged lover. He was taking a shower and when the place went up he took off, hopping, I guess."

"Must've been a hell of a case," I muttered. "What I'm saying, Chloe, is what if the extra tooth didn't belong to the victim?"

"What are you saying, there's a tooth fairy?"

"All his premolars were in place. Even after he hit the steering wheel."

"Of course they were. Your premolars are in the side of your mouth. They don't get knocked out like a canine or incisor. It only takes a moderately strong frontal blow. But your premolars and molars . . ."

"Exactly. So I'm asking, what will they do with the extra tooth?"

"I hope they send it to me. You can tell a lot from a tooth. Different materials have been used for fillings over the years. And as far as tooth morphology goes, American Indians—"

"—have shovel-shaped incisors. I know. You'll look at the tooth?"

"Sure. As soon as we finish with this body from the train wreck. The tank car exploded and—"

"Right. I'll see if I can get them to send it along."

"Great. Later, Alan."

I hung up and then called Willie Dupont and told him to try to get the pathologist to send the odd tooth to Chloe. When I'd finished talking to him I sat back in my chair and stared idly through my open door and into the next room, where I saw David's briefcase on the floor next to the sorting table. I wondered if he'd come back for it. Two hours later, when he hadn't returned, I called his house to see if he wanted me to drop it by on my way home, but his wife told me he hadn't come home. Maybe, I thought, he'd hit pay dirt with Absalom. At least I hoped so, because it would save us a lot of work. I closed the office and set the alarm, thinking of the empty house on Park Boulevard where I'd grown up and where I now lived.

Since returning to Baton Rouge I'd dated many women, and been serious about several. Some were taken by the old house with its antique furniture, but a few had told me how they'd change the decor. The latter I'd given short shrift, and as for the former, well, I'd managed to find something wrong with them, too. In a word, I was used to being alone, but sometimes—just sometimes—as when I spoke to David's wife, Elizabeth, and sensed the happiness of their relationship, I felt hollow.

It had been ten years since the dig at Oxmul, in Mexico. Ten years since I'd been a rising young archaeologist at the University of New Mexico. Ten years since Felicia and I had worked at one of the most important Maya sites ever discovered. Ten years since things with Felicia had gone to hell.

There was only one thing to do in such circumstances: I went home, changed into my shorts, put Digger on a chain, and after a few nominal stretching exercises, set out with Digger by my side to make the four-mile run around the lakes.

As we thudded down the hill on the bicycle path, and alongside the golf course, other joggers passed us. Most were younger than I, a few older. Some gave me a nod, others gazed straight ahead with that transfixed stare of the True Runner. They were the kind who jogged in thunderstorms and in the midday heat of summer. Even now, they were oblivious to the sweat soaking their shirts and running down their limbs.

I would never be like them: I was well into my forties and my brown hair was thinning. I had long ago accepted that I would only be average in height, and it was a constant struggle to keep my weight in the acceptable range. I wore glasses, and the prescription had been getting stronger over the years. For me, jogging was a duty, something I did both to get my mind off things I didn't want to think about, and to keep my weight under control. I got no joy from this mortification of the body, and had little regard for those fanatics who raced by in states of altered reality. It was, I told myself, a cult, and as a freethinker—

My stomach tightened as I saw a figure headed toward us, easily loping at about half the speed of sound.

A woman, long-legged, blond, in yellow shorts and a white jogging tank top with the number 12 on it. No glasses, no attaché case, but there was no doubt . . .

P. E. Courtney.

I increased my pace without thinking, and as we closed she gave me a friendly wave. I nodded, painfully aware of my snaillike speed. I gritted my teeth until she was past and then allowed myself to slow down, gulping air. Digger, meanwhile, had taken to the stepped-up pace and was tugging me forward. I started to give his chain a jerk and then heard steps bearing down on me from behind.

"Hi," a woman's voice said. "Do you usually walk this time of day?"

Walk . . .

"Sometimes," I mumbled, as she slowed to my own speed.

"That's good," she said. "A little more and you'll be in shape."

I started to reply, but she danced in a circle around me like a boxer before I could think of anything.

"Goodbye," she said, and I heard her steps dying away.

Damn. She hadn't broken a sweat.

An hour later I dragged myself out of the stifling humidity, shut the door, and collapsed into my easy chair. Digger headed for the kitchen to lap water from the pan I kept on the floor, and I went to the shower. Once I'd changed into shorts and a T-shirt, I went back to the living room and flipped on the TV. It was just after six, time for the local news. The silver-haired anchorman was just mentioning an escape from the state prison at Angola when Digger launched himself across the telephone table and, with both paws on my lap, proceeded to lick my face to remind me about his supper.

I heaved myself up, went into the kitchen, and opened him a can, then coaxed him out into the backyard with it.

I got out some of the burned jambalaya, stuck it in the microwave, and settled down before the TV again with a glass of iced cappuccino.

By that time, the news was over and a boyish-looking weatherman was pointing to a map of the state and explaining that it would stay hot and dry for the next few days, with temperatures in the nineties. I wasn't paying much attention to him, though, because I was still burned about running into the Courtney woman.

She'd thought I was *walking* . . .

I ate, went to bed early, and dreamed of watching her sink up to her preppie armpits in the gumbo mud that formed the land surface for the southern part of our state. She kept calling for me to throw her a line and I kept replying that I was too decrepit to get the rope out that far.

It was an eminently satisfying dream.

FIVE

I arrived at the office just before eight and the phone was already ringing. I yanked it up, mildly aggravated that whoever it was couldn't wait for me to sit down.

"Yes?"

"Alan, this is Elizabeth. I've been trying to get you all night, but the phone company said your phone was out of order."

I blanked for a second, then remembered Digger's lurch at me across the telephone table. It wouldn't be the first time he'd knocked it off the hook.

"I'm sorry. Look, what's wrong? Is David okay?"

"That's just it," she explained. "He never came in."

Something cold stole over me.

"You haven't heard from him?"

"No. Oh, my God, I was hoping you were together."

"Elizabeth, you should have come over."

"I was baby-sitting for friends. They went to New Orleans and I said I'd stay over night. I called David at nine and when he didn't answer, I called you. But I didn't start to really worry until I woke up and couldn't get either one of you. There must have been a wreck."

"Maybe his car broke down," I comforted. "But most of that road is four-lane. And it's only thirty miles."

"But what could have happened?"

I exhaled. No ready answer came to mind.

"Liz, all I can think is that he broke down and there

44

wasn't a phone. But, look, David and I've been in a lot of spots together. He can handle himself.''

"But I know he'd call."

"There has to be some reason. I'm leaving right now to go up there." I didn't tell her I'd also check with the sheriff's office and State Police.

"I could come," she offered, voice unsteady. "I mean, I could call into work . . ."

"Better you go on to your job. I'm betting it'll turn out to be nothing. And I'll call you as soon as I find him."

I scribbled a note to Marilyn and went back out to my red '86 Blazer. I'd told the truth about David and me being in tight places before, and the dents in the Blazer's body proved it. But there'd never been a case where he'd set out to go thirty miles and disappeared. It gave me a feeling I seldom had, one that I didn't especially enjoy.

I drove home first to check my phone. Sure enough, it was off the hook, where Digger had lurched at me. He was pawing on the back door now, hoping we were going for a ride, but I didn't have time to explain, so I threw him a Milk Bone and headed back out.

The morning rush hour was still on, and as I raced up the ramp to the freeway I had to slow for a pickup truck loaded with mattresses, lumbering along in the right lane. The white Acura Integra behind me would probably whip across the caution reflectors at the end of the on ramp to get past us both, and I squeezed the wheel, ready. But nothing happened. I fitted in neatly and the Integra took its time as well.

It was hard for me to imagine that there were people in the world who faced this traffic every morning.

By the time I came down off the interstate, at the north edge of the city, the traffic had evaporated, though I noticed the Integra was still back there. Now we had a four-lane straightaway for almost twenty miles, past the evil-smelling refinery, past the Civil War site of Port Hudson, all the way to Thompson Creek, which cuts across the base of the hills and divides the first terrace of the Mississippi from the loess bluffs for which Natchez is famous.

As I went, I kept my eye out for wrecked or abandoned Landcruisers, but David's vehicle was not on the side of the highway. At Thompson Creek, I even pulled over and got out to look down into the creek itself, but all I saw was a family picnicking.

That was when I noticed the Integra had stopped a hundred yards behind me. I stared at it for a second, tempted to walk back and ask if I was being followed, but then I told myself that David's disappearance had given me a dose of paranoia.

I left the four-lane and climbed into the hills then, overtaking a milk truck without much room to spare. The turnoff to the Dupont property was just ahead and I shot past it. A couple of miles further on, at a convenience store, I whipped into the parking lot and turned around. As I nosed back into the southbound lane, I saw the Integra coming up fast and caught a look of astonishment on the driver's face.

And I'm sure she saw the annoyed look on mine.

P. E. Courtney.

I didn't know what kind of game she was playing, but I knew I could shake her now, because by the time she got turned around I'd have vanished down the side road."

Why the hell was she following me, though? Nosiness? Or was it something more sinister? Could she have something to do with David's disappearance? Was Freddie St. Ambrose involved? It seemed unlikely: Freddie would screw you on a business deal, but he was not known for his physical prowess. His style was to sit in his air conditioning and make trouble over the phone. Still, David was gone. And it didn't help to know that T-Joe had died not far from where David had said he was going.

I wheeled right, off the highway, and floored it as I arrowed down the tar top, toward the river. She'd be back down on the four-lane before she figured out that she'd lost me, and by that time she'd have passed three or four places I might have turned.

I came out of a turn and braked. A quarter-mile ahead something—a car, it looked like—was blocking the road. My heart started into free fall. As I neared, though, I saw it was a sheriff's vehicle, with a deputy standing beside it to halt traffic.

A wreck. My God, he'd gone off the road into the ditch and they hadn't found him until this morning . . .

But then I saw that standing with the deputy were a couple of men in navy blue uniforms with red trim. The men held shotguns.

I slowed to a halt and the deputy plodded over to peer into my car.

"Morning, sir. You got business back here?"

One of the men in dark blue had taken up a position on the other side, and was eyeing my passenger compartment.

"I'm working for the Duponts," I said. "They bought some land back here from Greenbriar Plantation."

The deputy nodded.

"Something the matter?" I asked.

"Couple of inmates broke out of Angola yesterday," the deputy said, spitting in the road. "You seen anybody suspicious? Hitchhikers, say?"

I shook my head. "No. But isn't this a little far south? They'd have to have gone twenty miles, not to mention passing St. Francisville."

The man on the other side of my vehicle came around the front. He was beefy, with rings under his eyes. The patch on his shoulder said *Louisiana State Penitentiary*.

"Stole a boat," he said sourly. "We found it half a mile upstream. They probably snuck past St. Francisville last night, when the ferry wasn't working. Then the current put 'em ashore down here. We've got the chase team on the power plant grounds."

"I'll keep a lookout," I said. "By the way, have you seen a man in a brown Toyota Landcruiser? He was supposed to be working up near Greenbriar. He's one of my people."

The guard shook his head and the deputy looked blank. They'd both stepped back to let me pass when I saw them staring over my shoulder and I heard a car stopping behind me. I turned my head and froze: the Integra.

I walked back to her car and jerked her door open, almost spilling her into the road.

"Get out of the car," I said. "I want to find out what's going on."

Her mouth went open in surprise, and a few seconds later the deputy was standing next to me.

"What's going on?"

I turned to face him. "This woman's been following me from Baton Rouge."

He looked at me, then at her, and then back at me.

"And you're complaining?"

"One of my people is missing."

"I don't know anything about that," she said.

"You think she had something to do with it?" the deputy asked. The two guards were now standing beside him, grateful for the break in the monotony.

"I know I keep running into her," I said and realized as soon as I'd said it how weak it sounded.

"I'll trade places with you," the second guard said.

"This is harassment," I protested. "She followed me from Baton Rouge."

The deputy spat in the roadway again, then leaned down until his face was close to hers.

"Miss, you carrying a gun or a knife?"

"Of course not."

"You mean any harm to this man?"

"No."

The lawman straightened up and shrugged.

"Well, I don't see I can stop her from driving down a public road."

"Thank you," she said with a sweetness of which I'd never have thought her capable. I wheeled and walked back to the Blazer.

"Be careful and don't pick up anybody," the deputy called after me. "Same for you, ma'am. If you know each other, it'd be a good thing to travel together . . ."

But I was already driving away.

She stayed behind me all the way to Absalom Moon's shack. But by then I didn't care about her, because what I saw when I slowed to pull into his yard sent fear rippling through me: A brown Landcruiser was parked next to the chicken house. There was no sign of movement from the house as I stopped in the yard.

David had been here but the place looked deserted.

Six

I walked over to the Landcruiser, dimly aware that the Integra was pulling into the yard after me. I put my hand on the hood: *cold.*

"What's going on?" I heard her call, as she crossed the yard toward me. Another power outfit, white slacks with a black coat.

"Maybe you can tell me," I said acidly. "You've been following me all day."

"I was headed over to your office to talk to you," she said, her tone defensive. "I wanted to see if you'd heard any more about the Tunica job. I mean, since T-Joe Dupont got killed."

"You know about that?"

"I read the paper. So what's going on? Did he sign the contract before he died?"

"We're working for the family," I said. "But you still didn't say why you were here."

"I thought maybe I could help," she said.

"I never made any agreement to work with you," I told her. "I never said I'd cut you in on any of my business. And following me around sure as hell doesn't make me any more likely to work with you."

"I saw you leaving and I didn't know what to do, so I followed." She gave a little shrug. "It was just an impulse."

"And that's why you happened to run into me jogging yesterday?"

"That was an accident. I always jog there. I was glad to see you out walking. It's good for you."

"Out walking—" I cut myself off. "Look, let me make this short and sweet: I've worked without you for ten years. Believe it or not, there're plenty of people besides you who know something about the archaeology of these parts. I don't intend to subcontract you, especially not now. Not if you were the last archaeologist on earth."

She flinched at my words, or maybe it was just the sunlight in her eyes. I started to turn around and head up onto the porch, but her voice caught me:

"Alan, you *need* me," she said.

I stared at her. "What?"

"I'm an expert on contact period artifacts. I studied under the best. You're good, but you're a specialist in prehistory. Only 20 percent of the projects you've done have involved sites with a major historic component, and almost none of those have been contact period."

"How do you know all that?" I asked.

She folded her arms and looked me in the eyes.

"Do you think I'm a total idiot? I told you I did an analysis. After I decided I liked Louisiana, I settled on Baton Rouge instead of New Orleans because Baton Rouge is the capital and the state's archaeology bureaucracy is here, as well as the state university. There are also three viable contract archaeology firms. I researched every one of them. Don't you think I talked to people before I came down here? Freddie St. Ambrose is a sleaze. That's his reputation. I knew CEI did good work, and I knew you, though smaller than CEI, did good work, too. One day two months ago I flew down here and spent two days in the Division of Archaeology, checking their report files for who did what. That's how I know your track record."

"I'll be damned."

"I even saw you come into the office one of those days, to talk to Morgan. You were upset about one of your reports he'd reviewed."

My mouth must have come open a couple of inches. I vaguely recalled that a woman had been sitting at one of the big tables in the reading room, her head buried in some reports. I'd been more concerned that day with protesting a written comment one of the archaeology police had made about our shovel-testing regime.

Maybe, I told myself, P. E. Courtney wasn't a *total* loss.

"I want to work *with* you, not against you," she said.

It didn't make much sense to argue the point in a barn-yard.

"You can help me if you can tell me where David Goldman is," I said. "That's his Landcruiser. Nobody's seen him since yesterday. He came here to talk to the man who lives in this house. And he never came back."

P. E. Courtney frowned. "People don't just disappear," she said.

I started up the steps to the rickety porch. "No?" I pounded on the door frame. "Mr. Moon? Are you in there? This is Alan Graham. We met yesterday."

The front door was open, revealing a torn screen that allowed me to look down the hallway that ran the length of the dwelling. It was too dim inside for me to make out the interior, and I hesitated to go into someone's home without permission. If Absalom had been here he'd surely have been outside by now.

"You don't think they were both kidnapped," she said. "By those convicts, I mean."

I shrugged. I didn't know *what* to think. But there were beginning to be too many coincidences: the death of T-Joe, the escape of the two convicts, David's disappearance.

"I think it's time to call the sheriff," I told her.

She nodded. "Do you want to use your phone or mine?"

I took my flip phone out of my Blazer and she eyed it with disdain.

"Yours is bigger than mine," she said, and produced a telephone the size of a cigarette pack.

"It's called the Old Archaeology."

"I'm not trying to be confrontational," she said. "You can use my phone."

If it hadn't been important to find David I'd have told her what was on my mind. Instead, I waited while she got first Directory Assistance and then the number of the West

Feliciana Sheriff's Office. When the connection was complete, she handed the phone to me.

I got a woman deputy who told me that if my friend's car was where he'd left it, then the escaped cons obviously hadn't taken it and he was probably somewhere in the area. "Was he hunting out of season?" she asked.

"No, he was an archaeologist," I told her.

"Oh." Silence, then: "I didn't know there were any dinosaurs in this parish."

I tried to stay calm. "Look, he's not here, his vehicle's parked and hasn't been used for hours. He loves that Landcruiser. He wouldn't leave it. Add to that, there're two convicts loose. Doesn't that bother you?"

"Yes, sir. But most of our deputies are out there anyhow, with the search team. I'll tell them to be on the lookout. Can you give me his description?"

I told her what he looked like and how he'd been dressed. She repeated it all carefully.

"We'll put out a bulletin," she said and I thanked her.

"Now what?" P. E. Courtney asked.

"There's a house right over there," I said, pointing to the frame house next door. "I think I'll drive over and ask if anybody's seen anything. Maybe you want to wait here in case David shows up."

"Why don't *you* wait?" she asked sweetly. "He knows you. Besides, with convicts loose, they'd be more likely to talk to a woman than a man."

I threw up my hands. "All right, I'll leave a note on his windshield and we'll *both* go."

"My car or yours?"

"Mine," I answered, thinking at least that way I'd keep some control.

"Right. You *do* have insurance, don't you?"

"What?" My fists balled.

"I just mean your car's red. That usually indicates a flamboyant personality—traffic tickets and all that."

I exhaled slowly. "It can also indicate somebody who got a good deal on a slightly used Blazer that happened to be red."

"Oh," she said and went to lock up her vehicle.

I speculated on how long it would take the two convicts to break into the Integra and crack the steering column.

We nosed out onto the two-lane, and a hundred yards later turned into the yard of the white frame house with the satellite dish. Before we were out of the Blazer a man appeared on the screened porch. He had a pump shotgun in his hands.

"Who is it?" he called. "Just stand right there where I can see you."

We halted.

"My name's Alan Graham," I called. "I'm from Baton Rouge. We just want to ask you some questions."

The screen door opened and I saw the man in the sunlight for the first time. He was thin, with rimless glasses and white hair frosting the sides of his head. The sun danced off a bald skull, and there was a snake tattoo on his right forearm.

"What about?" the man demanded.

"We're archaeologists," I said. "The Dupont family hired us to look over their property for artifacts."

"You work for T-Joe?" He shook his grizzled head and lowered the gun. "Hell of a thing, what happened."

"You were here?"

"No. I saw it on my way back from St. Francisville. Was it a heart attack?"

"His son thinks it may have been murder."

"Murder? That don't make no sense."

"No," I said. "Look, Mr.—"

"Marcus Briney." He leaned the shotgun against the steps, next to a pair of hunting boots, and came over to shake my hand. He was dressed in a white T-shirt and khaki pants that looked like they'd just come out of the dryer. "Sorry about the twelve gauge. There's a couple of inmates on the loose and everybody's kinda spooked."

I told him my name. "And this is P. E. Courtney," I said.

"P. E.?" he asked. "What kind of name is that?"

"Mine," P. E. said icily.

"It stands for Prudence Elvira," I explained. "That's why she's sensitive."

"Oh." He chuckled. "I understand."

I watched P. E. turn red and go rigid all over.

"We're looking for a friend," I said. "Fellow named David Goldman." I pointed toward Absalom's house. "He came up here yesterday afternoon to talk to your neighbor, Absalom Moon, and he never came back. His Landcruiser is still in Absalom's yard."

Marcus Briney laughed.

"I wouldn't worry. Absalom probably took your friend off in the woods. He's a funny old nigger. If he doesn't like you, he won't give you the time of day. But if he takes a shine to you, he'll do anything in the world."

"It's strange they'd be gone all night and all day," I said.

Briney gave a little shrug. "Absalom knows these woods backward and forward. They may've camped out. And if there was any kinda problem, like falling down, Absalom can handle it."

"What about convicts?" I asked.

The old man stroked his chin. "Those fellows are probably on the nuclear plant grounds, from what I heard. My son's a guard lieutenant. He said the hounds picked up a scent this morning. They oughta have 'em by noon."

"Who are they?" P. E. asked then. "Do you know?"

"One's a white boy named Peterson, up for robbery. Other one's a nigger named Green, in for killing somebody in a dope deal. Don't know either one of 'em, though it seems like I was still there when Peterson got sent up."

"You were there?" P. E. asked.

Marcus Briney nodded. "I was assistant warden. Started as a guard and worked my way up. That's what all our family's done, ever since they put the prison there a hundred years ago. My father was one of the first guards hired on, after the state took over the place from the old plantation. Couldn't make it farming and took a job as a guard. Things were tough back then." He chuckled. "Tough times and tough men, on both sides of the fence. Prisoners excaped and was never heard from again." He gave a tight little smile. "Some of 'em didn't ex-cape and they still wasn't heard from again. In the old days they wasn't so particular about nose counts, know what I mean." He kicked at the dirt. "I was seven years old when my father got killed in the big breakout in '33. The guards chased those guys all the way across the river and caught up with some of 'em in Avoyelles Parish. Shot 'em dead on the spot. One of 'em they never caught. And you know what happened to the ones they brought back alive?"

I shook my head.

"Parish grand jury wouldn't indict 'em because they didn't figure it was the parish's business to spend money on a trial that ought to be paid for by the state." He scratched absently at his tattoo. "Now ain't that something?"

"It's something all right," I said.

"But, you know, it's the life we've got up here," the old man rambled. "I mean, whole families work at the prison. It's a way of life. Most of 'em live up near Tunica. When I retired, I decided to move down here. I love this land, but that part of my life was over. Why try to stay on and be a part of it?"

"Makes sense," I said. "Well, I guess we'll go look around Absalom's yard, see if we find any clues."

"You don't want to come in for some iced tea?" Briney asked.

"Thanks," I answered. "Another time."

I started away, then turned.

"By the way, I was talking to Carter Wascom yesterday, and he seemed to think there was some kind of plot to keep him from telling the truth about the bayou pollution."

Briney rasped out a laugh. "Yeah. Carter probably thinks Martians kidnapped Elvis."

"You think Carter could kill anybody?"

Another laugh. "Carter? Did you look at his hands? He never touched nothing rougher than a silk bedsheet." He lifted his own gnarled hands. "Not like these."

"You've killed people?"

"You're damn straight. In the war. And if those inmates come around I won't blink an eye."

"Well, nice talking with you, Mr. Briney."

"Same here, Mr. Graham. You, too, Miss Prudence," he said.

She spun on her heel and was closing the door of the Blazer before I reached it.

"Old geezer," she muttered. "Racist."

"Him or me?"

"Very funny. I especially liked the Prudence part."

"Well, what *does* the P. E. stand for?"

"None of your business."

I pulled up next to the Integra.

"Well, it'll take more than you or me to keep old-timers up here from saying *nigger*," I told her.

"Spare me the sociology lesson," she said, getting out.

"I'd as soon spare you, period," I muttered.

"Where are you going?"

"To look around the yard. David's missing, remember?"

I left her staring at my back and went around the house. There was no telling when the sheriff's department would get here, if ever, and it wouldn't hurt to see what I could turn up.

"Wait a minute," she called after me. "I'll help."

"I can't possibly see how," I said under my breath.

The yard behind the house told me nothing. The grass was mostly gone, and chickens flapped away as I approached. The footprints of several people mingled in the dirt, but I couldn't tell whose they were. At the rear of the yard, entwined in vines and high grass, was the rusted hulk of a sixties-vintage Fairlane. I peered inside but there was nothing of interest. Then, to the side of the car, I saw a path heading into the forest. There were foot marks indicating someone had used the trail, but I wasn't enough of a tracker to know whether it had been a day or a week ago.

"Where are you going?" P. E. asked.

"There's a trail. I thought I might walk in a little ways. You'd better stay here, with those high heels."

"Just a minute." She went back to the Integra and I saw her reaching behind the seat. She dropped something onto the ground and stepped out of her shoes. Then she took off the black jacket and locked it in the car.

"Now," she said as she came across the yard. I saw

she'd changed the spike heels for flats. So the girl had *some* sense . . .

I started down the little trail, ducking under the low branches. If they'd come this way, David had been hit in the face by tree limbs just as I was being hit. There was an especially low one ahead, and as I bent under it the notebook slid out of my pocket and fell onto the ground.

When I stooped to pick it up, my hand froze halfway down.

Beside it, in the dirt, was a mechanical pencil of the kind I'd seen David use in the office, in his drafting.

Now there was no doubt: He'd come this way.

SEVEN

    I lunged forward, eyes searching the ground for more clues. He'd been on this path, and that probably meant he was somewhere in these woods. I'd gone another hundred feet when I heard her calling out behind me:

"Wait."

I halted. So she was finding the going a little tough, was she?

"If you can't keep up—" I started but she cut me off:

"Don't you think it would be a good idea to have a map?"

I turned around slowly, sweat dripping from my forehead.

"I don't have a map," I said, angry that she'd caught me out. "Do you?"

"In my car," she said. "I'll be back in a minute."

And she was gone. I stood in the shade, brushing a mosquito away from my eyes, and wondered what she'd come back with. A map of the plantation trail, maybe, issued by the West Feliciana Chamber of Commerce . . .

When ten minutes had passed I decided she couldn't find it and was relieved. Then I heard the brush crackling and a figure in designer jeans and cotton work shirt emerged, carrying a map tube and a small backpack.

I must have gaped because she felt it necessary to explain:

"I thought I ought to change clothes if we're going to make an expedition out of this." She eyed my slacks and guayabera. "Don't you have any clothes in your Blazer?"

"These'll do," I muttered.

"Fine. You want me to lead?"

"That's okay." I preceded her down the trail. There was deer sign and once I saw a spent shotgun shell, but it could have been there for six months. Twenty minutes after we started, the trail ended at a gully. The sides were hung with kudzu and at the bottom, fifteen feet below, was a narrow stream. I bent to study the edge and saw undeniable scuff marks.

"Somebody climbed down here," I said.

She unscrewed the top of the plastic map tube and drew out a rolled-up topographic sheet.

"We're right here," she said, pointing at a dashed blue line that cut through high hills.

I nodded. "I think you're right." My eyes went west on the map, to where, just beyond the next ridge, the land fell into a flat coastal plain a mile wide that ended at the river. Part of the plain appeared detached from the mainland by another dashed line, like a barge anchored against the shore. A few jeep trails showed as broken lines on the green paper. It was a lot of territory to cover. My better judgment told me to go back, wait for the law. But, damn it, with all the deputies tied up in the search for convicts, it could be hours before they mounted a search, and meanwhile David was out there.

"I'm going down," I said.

"Do you want me to go first?" she asked, and I could tell she was serious.

"I can manage," I told her. "Just wait here at the top and then you can follow me."

I grabbed a tree root and lowered myself gingerly, hunting for a foothold against a small sapling part of the way down. The soil was wet from being in the shade and as I transferred my weight to the small tree I felt my foot starting to slip. I reached for a branch hanging out over the chasm and felt it bend. My foot slipped away from the sapling and I fought to regain my purchase. I wedged my foot between the tiny trunk and the bluff and then, to my horror, felt the sapling give way. I plunged down but something caught my free hand.

"Hang on," P. E. Courtney said.

I lashed out with my foot, found a small niche in the soft earth, and then launched myself over to where I could grab another root. This time the root held and I was able to lower myself to the bottom of the gully.

I looked down at my slacks: They were smeared with red clay, and water was seeping into my shoes. Worst of all, P. E. Courtney was picking her way down as daintily as a veteran rock climber.

A few seconds later she landed beside me, on the wet gravel.

"Oh," she said. "You have on low quarters. Your feet are getting wet."

I looked down: She'd changed footwear again, this time to low hiking boots.

"It's happened before," I said. "Look."

She stared down where I was pointing. It was a pair of deep impressions, now filled with water.

"Somebody crossed here," I said.

"Your friend?"

"I don't know."

But it had to be. And as I searched the gravel on this side I saw other marks, too many for one person.

Either he'd been following someone or they'd been following him.

I considered the steep face of the gully opposite.

"He couldn't have gotten up there," I said. "He has to have followed the stream to a place where the banks were lower."

"You want to split up and each take a direction?" she asked.

I shook my head. "We stick together. One lost person is enough."

"I have a compass," she said.

"Good," I growled. "Because I don't."

Not that we'd need it following a stream. But I didn't like what I was feeling about this place. And I was beginning to think maybe P. E. Courtney might be able to handle herself in the woods after all.

We followed the little trickle north, the bluffs on our right side. My feet crunched into the gravel, and a couple of times I had to step quickly to keep from sinking. I no longer saw any more boot marks and began to wonder if I'd made the right decision: What if he *had* gone the other way, toward the confluence of the two streams? And the truth came to me suddenly: He hadn't had a map, so, of course, there was no way he could have known.

Damn. She'd been thinking straight and I hadn't. Why the hell hadn't she said something? Was she just being nice, catering to my male ego? P. E. Courtney didn't seem the type, yet . . .

The sound of a limb breaking tore my thoughts back to the here and now. A huge bough came crashing toward us and I lunged against her, driving her away from the danger. A half-second later the great limb landed in the water two feet away, showering us with droplets.

"My God," she said, getting up slowly from the gravel verge. "I didn't even see that thing . . ."

Maybe it was the fear in her eyes, but for the first time I thought I detected a crack in her East Coast veneer.

I reached out a hand to help her up and she took it, then, as she steadied herself, let go quickly and started to brush herself off as if she were afraid some telltale trace of weakness might still cling to her.

Now I looked down at the piece of wood that had almost killed us.

"I didn't hear the limb break," she said. Then, seeing me staring at it, she took a step closer: "What's wrong?"

"You didn't hear it because it didn't break," I said. "At least, not just now. Look at the ends."

They were fungus-covered. The huge trunk had been lying on the ground above, long enough to be infested with rot.

"Let's get out of here," I said under my breath.

"What?"

That was when we heard the crackle of sticks breaking somewhere on the edge of the cliff above us.

I grabbed her hand and jerked her forward. *"Now!"*

Soil was cascading down from where someone stood on the edge above us, hidden by the forest shadows.

"I don't guess you've got a gun in there someplace," I said, nodding at her pack.

She shook her head. "Sorry."

The footsteps were definite now, crunching the dead leaves and twigs of the forest overhead. I searched the defile in front of us for a way to go, but there was no choice except forward.

At that second another log came crashing down from above and I grabbed P. E. and pulled her after me into the streambed. The cold water filled my shoes, but that was the least of my concerns: If we stayed close to the bluff on the right, we were prey for whatever got thrown down on us, but here, out from under the edge, we could be picked off by a gun.

"This way," I said, pointing ahead. We ran upstream to a place where the left bank was low and she scrambled up it easily. I followed and, touching the grass on the top, crawled behind a log.

The echoes of our splashes died away and gradually the sounds of the forest returned to normal. I pointed at the cliff face across from us.

"They'll play hell getting down that."

"So what do we do?" she asked. "We need to get out of here and get help."

"Where's your phone?" I asked.

She fished it out of her pocket and punched in 911.

Only static.

I watched her put it away, chagrined. "I say we go to the island and hike out on one of the jeep roads the map shows. Whoever that was will probably go back."

And, I thought, we would be leaving David to whatever had happened to him. But there was nothing to be done; two lost people couldn't help a third.

For a moment longer I watched the leafy curtain across the creek, and then I scrambled backward on hands and knees until I was completely in shadow and got slowly to my feet, P. E. following.

She pulled out the map tube, which she'd had slung across her back on a cord. "Here's where I think we are," she said. "The hills should end the other side of this ridge, and then a quarter-mile and we're on the island."

I nodded. "And once we get there, there's a trail running down the middle."

"Right." She stowed the map and we started toward the edge of the ridge.

The side sloped at about forty degrees and I started down on my seat, sliding and skidding until I hit the bottom and came up on my feet. P. E. wasn't so lucky and rolled into an untidy heap. When I stretched out a hand to help her she ignored it and dragged herself upright.

"I think the island's that way," she said, pointing ahead of us.

We lurched through a stand of palmetto and I felt our feet sinking into the mud. We were out of the hills now and into the coastal plain. This had been an old course of the Mississippi, at a time when the first white men were taking this land from the Tunica and their kinsmen, and that was why no one really believed there was still a Tunica village to be found: The irresistible waters would have torn it away well over a century ago.

I stole a look at my watch. It was just after ten. We'd been in the woods for an hour and the heat was suffocating.

P. E. Courtney unslung her little backpack, reached into it, and withdrew a plastic water bottle.

I watched, incredulous, as she took a long swallow, then offered it to me.

"Water?" she asked sweetly.

"I'll go a little longer, thanks," I said, and then kicked myself mentally.

Just ahead of us was a bottom area, studded with jutting cypress knees. The surface was green with duckweed and I wondered if we dared try to cross. But before I could say anything, she was sloshing forward into the swamp, arms outstretched for balance. I started to call after her and realized it would do no good.

I saw the water reach her calves, then her thighs.

Grudgingly, I admitted I'd been wrong in my assessment

of her ability do to fieldwork. All I could do now was follow.

I tried to hurry, but the mud sucked at my feet and I felt like a man in a dream.

Twenty feet ahead of me, she was hauling herself up out of the water, though it looked like she'd found a briar patch for her landfall.

I wondered if she had a collapsible machete in her pack.

Somehow she found her way out of the briars and I followed, leaving bits and pieces of myself on the thorns. She waited, standing atop a tree stump, and took a reading with her compass.

"Straight ahead," she pronounced.

Who was I to argue?

The undergrowth grew thinner, and I saw with relief that the surface we walked on was becoming sandy. The smell of the river was heavy now, and I listened for the sound of waves or boats passing, but as yet there was nothing.

"Look," P. E. called, pointing. There was a lighter area ahead, where more sun fell through the trees, and I knew it had to be the path that ran from one end of the island to the other. A few seconds later I emerged onto the trail. It had been made by the jeeps and ATVs going to hunting stands. I would have given several portions of my anatomy for an ATV just now.

We reexamined the topographic sheet. The easiest way off the island was to follow the trail right, toward the tip, and then take what appeared to be a small bridge back across the bayou. If we did this, we would have a trek of half a mile across the floodplain and another mile or so through the hills on a winding track, before we hit the paved road, a mile north of where our cars were parked.

"Are you sure you don't want some water?" she asked.

This time I swallowed my pride and said yes.

I took a couple of gulps and forced myself to stop.

"Thanks." I handed the bottle back to her. The trees were thinner ahead of us and as we started toward them I saw a brightness that I knew was glare from the river. I made a straight line through the brush for the water, and emerged into the open. Below me erosion had etched gullies into the sand, from the bluff top to the water's edge. The water itself was brown, and here and there tiny mirrors of sunlight sparkled on the waves. The opposite bank, nearly a mile away, was a low tree line, riding a white belt of sand. I thought about the escaped convicts and how desperate Angola had made them that they were willing to brave thirty miles of river. They'd beached near here, according to the guards, and then, being creatures of dry land, had headed inland and away from the river with its mysterious depths and devilish currents.

I let myself down slowly onto the sand, and touched something eroding from the soil.

"What do you have, a cartridge case?" she asked.

I shrugged. "Brass."

"I've seen lots of it. This place must be a shooting gallery during hunting season."

"Must be," I agreed.

She peered down at me. "Say, are you going to make it? You look tired."

I started to tell her I'd dance at her funeral, but held my tongue. "I'm fine," I said.

"Are you sure?" She pulled the water bottle out of her pack: "Here. Take some. I don't want you having heat stroke."

I was still staring at the water bottle when the brush crackled behind her. She let the bottle fall from her hand and it went rolling down the slope toward the river. Suddenly dogs were baying and there was a din of men's voices and the crackle of radios. A man in camouflage green stepped from the trees, rifle in hand.

"What the hell are you people doing here?" he demanded in a gravelly voice.

EIGHT

I pulled myself to my feet.

Other armed men materialized from the trees. Most wore camouflage, but some were dressed in the dark blue with red trim that identified them as members of the prison guard force. A couple of bloodhounds strained at their leashes and the man holding them looked as if it wouldn't take much to let them loose.

"I asked you a question," the man with the gravelly voice said. "Who are you people and what are you doing here?"

"We're looking—" We started to answer together and then stopped. P. E. glanced at me and I began over.

"We're looking for a friend who disappeared yesterday. We went to Absalom Moon's place and found his car. It looked like he went into the woods."

The team leader cast a scornful look at my mud-spattered clothes. He was a wiry man with a baseball cap and sunglasses over a jutting jaw, and there were places on his cheek that his razor had missed.

"And you came back here dressed like that?" He nodded at P. E. "Hell, *she's* better dressed for the woods than you are."

P. E. managed a demure smile. "I don't think he always dresses like this in the field," she said sweetly, and I restrained myself from grabbing her neck.

"Listen," I said. "We've got to find my friend. There's somebody back here in the woods who tried to kill us."

The leader gave the man with the hounds a sideways look as if to confirm my insanity.

"What's your friend's name?" the first man asked.

"David Goldman," I said.

"Got his description?"

I tried to keep my temper. "He's thin, about thirty-five, dark hair, five-ten. Look, Mr.—"

But the man ignored me. Instead he unclipped a small radio from his belt and spoke into it. I didn't hear what he said because the hounds started baying. When they stopped the team leader was replacing his radio.

"Your friend's okay. He's at my old man's house, up on the road."

"Your old man?"

"Marcus Briney. They brought your buddy out an hour ago. He's okay except for a broke leg."

I heard the whinny of a horse and a man in uniform emerged from the woods, riding a chestnut mare. The mare did a little dance for us and the man pulled the reins, bringing her to a stop.

"Goodeau's gonna be pissed," he declared. "They was supposed to be on the nuclear plant grounds."

"Screw Goodeau," young Briney spat. "If he'd of been the kind of warden he was supposed to be they wouldn't of got out to start with."

"The escapees are in this area?" I asked.

Briney gave me a dark look. "Don't you worry none where those inmates are. If we hadn't been sidetracked with finding civilians we might of had 'em by now."

P. E. Courtney put her hands on her hips: "We have every right to be on our client's property."

I thought Briney was going to explode but before he could respond there was the distant thrum of helicopter rotors.

"Damn," he muttered.

The horse started to do her dance again, as the helicopter sound grew louder, and the hounds started to protest.

"That son-of-a-bitch," Briney cried, and I had the feeling he wasn't talking about either of us.

The chopper emerged over the trees now, coming from

the direction of the hills. It hovered over our heads for a few seconds, the draft from the blades whipping sand into our faces and making the horse rear up. Then it moved down the beach to a flatter spot and slowly settled. A few seconds later a short man in khakis popped out of the passenger side and ran toward us, hunched over.

The warden, Levi Goodeau.

"I heard you found tracks at the edge of the hills," he said. "You seen anything else since then?"

Briney shook his head. "No, sir. We were too busy rescuing civilians."

Goodeau squinted up at me. "I know you, don't I?"

I nodded and explained how we'd ended up here.

He shook his head. "Pretty risky, I'd say. I'll take you both back in the chopper. Your friend's okay." He turned to Briney. "I've asked for help from the State Police."

The younger man glowered. "Warden, we don't need no help from the State Police. We got six chasers on horses and four teams of hounds. I'll guarantee we run 'em down before dark. You know how it is in there: All we got to do is put on the pressure. After a while they'll give out and just wait for us to come."

Goodeau shook his head. "I think we'd better have the State Police," he said. "We can't take any more chances."

Briney started to protest, then turned away angrily. "Come on," he said to the others. We watched them disappear into the foliage.

"Old ways die hard," the warden observed. "Young Jack Briney's a good man, but they're still playing cowboys at Angola. It's hard to change." He smiled then, like a man pleased with himself. "But we're working on it."

We followed him back to the helicopter and he waited politely while we climbed in, P. E. first and then me. The warden followed, shutting the door, and when we'd strapped in, the engine roared and we began to rise. In a few incredible seconds the island took shape below us as a bumpy green mat with a brown band of river on one side and steep hills on the other. I caught the reflection of P. E.'s face in the Plexiglas and knew what she was thinking: That in the last hour and a half we'd blundered our way across that terrain and sunk up to our hips in swamp, but now, in a few short seconds, we were jumping over it.

She pointed then, and when I looked I saw the little creek where we'd been pursued. And once more I knew we were thinking the same thing: Who could have been trying to frighten us away? Not the convicts, because all they cared about was getting away. There was no reason for them to try to frighten away hikers who'd never even seen them. That only drew attention to themselves. No, it had to be someone else, someone who didn't want us there. But who? Marcus Briney? He'd hardly had time to put on field clothes and come after us, and I hadn't heard any steps following us into the brush.

Without thinking I let my hand reach down and touch the piece of brass in my pocket.

It had to be Absalom Moon. He hadn't seemed like a violent man, but you could never tell. He was protecting terrain he considered his, protecting what was there. That was the only conclusion I could draw.

As we reached the last rise, I looked over the sea of trees and saw the nuclear plant, tall stacks gleaming in the sun, parking lot dotted with cars. *They'd thought the two convicts were on the grounds, somewhere inside the chain-link fence. Now they were saying the men had doubled back to the river.* I filed the fact away for future reference. Below us, I saw Absalom's house, a tiny box on a brown scab of yard. Our cars had been joined by a couple of others, and as we settled downward I saw bodies milling about like black beetles. Down the road, at the house of Marcus Briney, there were even more vehicles, and I recognized an ambulance. My heart jumped: *They'd said David only had a broken leg.*

Two cars moved out of the yard then, one to block the road near Greenbriar and the other a quarter-mile north of Absalom's, and I realized they were preparing for the chopper to land on the tar top.

Heat from the black surface radiated up at us and the telephone wires trembled with the breath of our descent. A second later there was a bump and the warden swung open his door and hopped down. We followed, keeping our heads low, and when we were clear the rotor revved again and the big machine started to rise, hovering for a second over the roadway and then grinding west, toward the river.

There were a couple of deputies and a man in guard uniform in the front yard, and I saw that a pair of paramedics technicians were sliding a stretcher into the ambulance. There was someone on the stretcher, and as I approached I recognized David.

"It's about time," he said, smiling, when he saw me. His eyes went from me to the woman. He gave a little frown and I knew he was wondering how she'd managed to be here.

"What happened?" I asked, resting a hand on his shoulder. His clothes were torn and his face was a map of scratches. He gave a weak little shrug.

"I don't know, Alan. I came to see Absalom and for a few minutes it was going well. We talked about the Bible and the Book of Kings and I was even sitting on the front porch with him. But when I started asking him about the artifacts he jumped like I'd shot him."

The stretcher bumped going into the rear of the vehicle and David winced.

One of the paramedics, a big man with a handlebar mustache, started to close the ambulance door.

"We need to get him to the hospital. You can talk to him there. Any preference?"

"The Lake," I said. The paramedic nodded and I watched him get in and start to back out of the yard. They'd take him to Our Lady of the Lake, the Catholic Hospital in Baton Rouge. I knew that David, the ex-rabbinical student, would enjoy the irony.

The ambulance roared off and I saw that Warden Goodeau had struck up a conversation with Marcus Briney. As I approached, I heard Briney say, "The boy's always had cement in his head, Levi. I never could tell him a damn thing."

Goodeau stared down at the ground, abashed.

"I think it'll work out," he mumbled.

"Well," Briney opined, "it will or it won't. I'll tell you like Boss Ross used to tell me, 'Either I'm the warden or you are. There ain't two.' That boy of mine's got to make up his mind. If he can't, then you gotta do what's right.''

"It'll work," Goodeau said and turned around, embarrassed, when he saw I was listening. "Looks like your friend'll be all right," he said quickly.

"We'd still like to know what happened to him," P. E. said from my elbow. "Because whatever it was almost happened to us."

"Oh?" The two men, joined by a sheriff's deputy, were staring at us now.

A warning bell in my unconscious sounded. There were too many uncertainties to give out everything we knew . . .

"She means with convicts out there," I said. "They might've gotten us. I guess it was the convicts that did that to David, right?" From the corner of my eye I saw P. E. frown and I gave her a stern look, hoping it would silence her.

"Don't know," the warden said. "All I heard was that he got hurt. A fall, I think. But why he was out there is something else again."

Briney turned to the warden: "Anyway, I expect they'll run 'em to ground by nightfall. Always happens. Unless they take to the river again."

Levi Goodeau shook his head. "I hope they don't do that, Marcus. I don't think either one of 'em can fight those currents."

Briney's expression turned pensive. "That's true, Levi, but there's another way to look at it. When you take away a man's freedom, send him to work in the fields, and the rest of the world out there acts like he's dead . . ." Briney shrugged. "Sometimes he's better off."

Goodeau started to protest but the old man raised a hand:

"I spent forty years up there, Levi. I'm telling you, no matter how much you try to change things, sometimes the river is a mercy."

≡ NINE

It took four hours to finish the X-rays, set David's leg, and move him to a room. Meanwhile, I'd called Elizabeth and she'd come to the hospital to wait with us. I also called the office and let Marilyn know what had happened. To her credit, P. E. Courtney had refused to budge from the chair in the emergency waiting room, except when I insisted that we go to the cafeteria. People gave us odd looks, with our mud-spattered clothes, but she might as well have been wearing a Dior gown, for all the difference it seemed to make to her.

At just before three they called us to go up to his room. We let Elizabeth go first and trailed in after she'd embraced him and made the proper consoling chitchat. Then she stepped aside and David saw P. E. and me:

"I think the wrong person's in this bed," he said.

I managed a weak smile. "I feel like it."

He looked over at P. E. Courtney and gave a curt nod.

"P. E. and I sort of ran into each other up there," I explained. "When we couldn't find Absalom, we followed the trail into the brush and found your pencil on the ground. We thought you'd be nearby."

David grinned ruefully. "To tell the truth, I don't know *where* I was. When I started asking old Absalom about the artifacts, he said he had something to show me. He got up and went into his house and I thought he was rooting around for something to bring out. Then I heard the back door slam, so I got up and went around the house and saw him headed into the woods. I yelled after him but it didn't do any good. My mistake was in following him.''

''You ended up in the creek,'' I surmised.

''Exactly. I wasn't sure which way to go, so I headed north a little ways, because I thought I heard him splashing around ahead of me, but there weren't any tracks, so I turned around and started back in the other direction, south. I was looking so hard at the ground, to try to find his trail, I guess I passed where I came in without knowing it.''

I caught P. E.'s look: *I told you we should have gone south.*

David went on: ''I don't know how far I went. Probably a couple hundred yards. Then I was sure I heard something, like somebody above me, in the woods. I yelled but there wasn't any answer. Then somebody threw something, a big log, that landed in the water and scared hell out of me.''

Elizabeth gave a little gasp but neither P. E. nor I showed any surprise.

''I found a place to climb up the bank, on the west side, and headed toward the river. But when I started down the last slope I tripped on something, and as soon as I landed I knew my leg was broken. I dragged myself a hundred yards or so, because I hoped I could make it to a jeep trail, but I ended up just lying there, by the swamp, until the dogs found me.'' He shook his head. ''At first I thought the chase team was going to celebrate. But when they came and saw I wasn't one of their convicts I thought for a minute they were going to string me up.''

I looked at the mosquito bumps on his face.

''I guess it was a pretty long night,'' I said.

He jerked his head in assent. ''Damn right. When you're alone in the woods you hear all kinds of noises. Birds, wildcats, maybe even a coyote. But I had the damnedest sensation while I was lying there. It was about the only time in my life I've really felt creepy.''

''Oh?''

He wore an expression I'd never seen before, far from his usual self-confidence and cheerful cynicism.

''All I can say is it felt like somebody was out there watching.''

*   *   *

We stayed another few minutes and then left him with Elizabeth. I went home and washed a few pounds of dried, stinking gumbo mud off me, and rubbed Dr. Tichenor's antiseptic on my insect bites. Then I changed clothes and drove to the office to relay the news in person before Marilyn took my call to mean David was undergoing amputation. She almost ran into my arms, this tiny, usually self-possessed girl whom I'd hired to do our books when she was a student. But, fortunately for her self-esteem, she caught herself short.

"Is everything all right?"

"He'll be on crutches for a while," I said. "Besides that everything's okay."

"We'll have to file a workers' comp claim." She sighed. "They'll want all kinds of information. Our rates may go up."

"Then we'll have to pay them," I said and started into my office.

"Oh, Alan."

I turned around. "Yes?"

"Willie Dupont called. He wanted to talk to you. When I told him there'd been an accident he said he was driving over."

I nodded in resignation.

"And there was also a call from Marvin Ghecko."

I closed my eyes and told myself to count to ten. "What does he want?" I asked.

"He didn't say. But he wanted you to call when you got back."

Marvin Ghecko, the Acting State Archaeologist, was a five-foot, two-inch wisp whose office evaluated all reports on projects done under federal and state auspices. We called him Marvelous Marvin and Ghecko the Echo, the latter for his habit of repeating himself when he was agitated. Now I dialed his private line and wondered what I'd done to merit his concern.

He picked it up on the first ring.

"Dr. Ghecko," he said.

I took a deep breath.

"Marvin, this is Alan Graham."

"Oh, Alan, thank God you called. I need to talk to you like yesterday." He had a high-pitched voice, and I envisioned him perched on his padded chair with his thin sandy hair slicked down with a ton of grease, and his feet hanging inches above the floor.

"Today's the best I can do, Marvin."

"Look, what's this about you and some new Tunica Treasure, what is it, eh?"

Oh, God, I thought.

"Just rumors, so far," I said, trying to sound blithe. "We were hired to survey some land just south of the nuclear plant. The owner had heard there was a site on it."

"A site, eh? And have you found it yet?"

"No."

"Alan, listen: I don't have to tell you if you find some Tunica burial place the tribe is going to jump in with both feet. Both feet, Alan. Why didn't this landowner send us a request for clearance?"

"Because he isn't going to be disturbing any site, for one thing, Marvin. And for another, it's private land and he can do what he wants. And for the third thing, he's dead."

"Oh." There was silence while he mentally regrouped. "But if there's burials it's a whole new ball game. You should have called me as soon as this came up. I don't like being sucker-punched. Don't like it at all."

"Who hit you, Marvin? Freddie St. Ambrose? Is he pissed because he didn't get the job?"

"Can't divulge sources. Just say a little bird. But you really should have called."

"You're right." I sighed. "I'm sorry."

Marvin made a grunting sound of approval.

"So have you found anything yet?" he asked.

I thought of the little brass object in my pocket, that I'd picked up from the beach. It could have gotten to the island in a thousand different ways.

"Lots of mosquito bites," I said. "And David hurt his leg in a fall."

"Fall. Well, that's rough country. Rough," he repeated,

as if he'd actually worked there. "Look, you keep me in-
formed, aye? I need to know what's happening. I *am* the
State Archaeologist."

"*Acting* State Archaeologist, Marvin."

"What?" This time there was alarm in his voice. "Have
you heard something about the final selection? *You* didn't
apply for the job, did you?"

"They wouldn't ever choose me, Marvin. I'm too much
of a maverick."

"That's true enough. You had me scared for a minute.
Well, thanks for calling, Alan. I feel better now."

I wish I could have said the same for myself. Because
while I hadn't lied to him, I hadn't been perfectly candid,
any more than I had when P. E. had thought I'd picked up
a cartridge case and I'd let her believe it. What I was holding wasn't much bigger than my thumb and it was the kind
of artifact I'd seen many times in books and in museum
cases. It was a small brass bell of the kind that Europeans
had traded to Indians in the eighteenth century, along with
kettles, blankets, and glass beads. It was the kind of artifact
T-Joe had produced the day we'd met, the kind that formed
a tiny portion of the famous Tunica Treasure.

══ TEN

That afternoon I visited David again in the hospital. He had his color back and he was lying with his leg in a cast, propped up on pillows. Elizabeth, he explained, had gone home to get some things, but would come back to stay with him overnight.

"About the business in the woods," I said. "You told me you had the feeling somebody was out there watching you."

"That's right. And you know I'm not the kind to let their imagination run haywire. But somebody—or some*thing*—was definitely chasing me before I fell." He eyed me. "You can call me crazy if you want."

I shook my head and walked over to the window and looked out. Below, the tiny cars and antlike people were baking in the summer heat, but inside it was cool. I turned around to face him.

"I don't think you're crazy," I said. "The same thing happened to us."

He listened, amazed, as I told him how we had fled along the creek, while something on the bluff above had tossed logs down at us.

"There's something, or somebody, out there," I said. "And I don't have any idea who."

"Me either," he said, reaching for his water glass. "Except I can't see it being Absalom. He was too spooked. It was almost like he *knew* there was something to be scared of and that was why he didn't want any part of it."

"I know, but who else could it be?"

He shrugged. "There are those convicts. But it doesn't seem like they'd do something so obvious. If I was trying to run away, I'd lie low. Or else I'd kill somebody and take what they had. But I sure as hell wouldn't play hide-and-seek."

"Well, I never heard of a Sasquatch in these parts," I joked.

"No. It's almost like there's something somebody's trying to protect, so they're trying to run everybody off. But I didn't find anything, did you?"

My fingers closed around the little bell in my pocket and was pulling it out to show him when the door opened and Willie Dupont stood swaying in the entrance.

"I came as soon as I heard." He advanced into the room, bringing with him a strong smell of whiskey. "Is he okay?"

I motioned to David, in the bed.

"Ask him yourself."

Willie's face relaxed. "Man, you had me scared. I called up your office and that girl wouldn't tell me crap. But I could tell something was the matter. I called Carter Wascom and asked him had he seen you people, and he said somebody'd been hurt. So as soon as I could I took off for Baton Rouge."

"I'm okay," David said. "Maybe even better than you are."

Willie collapsed into the big easy chair.

"Things goin' to shit. Whole damn family's mad at me now. My sister Dominique thinks I'm trying to get the treasure for myself. She thinks it's worth a lot of money."

"Really." I couldn't think of anything else to say.

"But it isn't, is it? I mean, what you told Dad was right, it's just a historical sort of thing."

"That's right," I said.

"They're mad 'cause they couldn't bury him today." He took a pint bottle out of his pocket and started to pull on it, then realized it was empty and set it down hard on the floor. "They hate to admit I was right."

"What happened?" I asked.

"That doctor over here that did the autopsy: He says it was murder, too."

I felt a little chill ripple through me.

"Murder?"

"Damn straight: Somebody shot him in the back of the head, through the back window. Coroner didn't catch it right off 'cause the window was broke and the bullet hole was so small his hair covered it."

I thought of Carter Wascom and his carbine.

"What caliber?" I asked.

"Said it was a .22."

"Magnum?"

"Wasn't sure. The bullet broke in pieces."

He wiped a hand across his mouth and belched.

"So now the shit's in the fan. Mom's in bed and Dominique is going crazy, she's so sure I'm trying to pull a fast one. They don't want to know the truth. They just want it to all be done. Well, that ain't good enough. He was my father, damn it."

He staggered forward until his face was a few inches from my own.

"You know what I did when I was a junior in high school? Me and some friends broke into a hospital to get some dope. Got caught big as shit. I dragged my family through the courts. And you know what? My dad never stopped supporting me. As much as I shamed him I was still his son. Oh, he let me sit in jail a few months. Said it was something him and the judge worked out to teach me a lesson. But once I came out it was over with. That's the kind of man he was, and the bastard killed him is gonna pay."

"Did the pathologist send the tooth to Chloe Messner?" I asked.

"I had to threaten the son-of-a-bitch. Said he didn't know what she could say about it, that it wasn't from Dad's mouth, so what was there to do with it?"

Professional jealousy. I'd seen enough of that before.

"Yeah. So I was thinking about the project. Ain't worth getting nobody else killed."

"No," I said. "But I'd like to have a little more time to work on it. We'll take precautions."

I didn't add that I didn't have the foggiest notion what kind.

"And then there's those damn convicts," he said. "Have they caught 'em yet?"

"Not yet," I said. "But they always do."

"Sure, but meanwhile . . ." He shrugged. "Look, have you all found anything so far?"

"No archaeological deposits," I said truthfully. "We were hoping Absalom could help us more."

Willie shook his head. "I don't know what's wrong with that man," he said. "Carter told me *Absalom*'s turned up missing, too."

He wove to the other side of the room. "My sister said I was throwing money down the drain, that Absalom probably found those things ten miles away, that nobody ever wanted that land for anything but hunting, that's why Carter sold it to us, because he saw a dumb coonass who didn't know what land around here was worth. Then she turned around and said I was trying to swindle her. She's held it against me ever since I had my problem with the law. Like I don't know what I did to the folks. Now she figures I've got some other reason for going through with it. Families!"

He turned an anguished face to my own. "Dad had it all worked out: the nature trails, picnic spots, the lake. He was gonna make our own little piece of paradise right here. He ended up dead because of it."

"I still think it's a good dream," I said quietly.

"Dream," he repeated. "That's what it was, all right. A daydream nobody in their right mind would've had."

"It isn't over," David argued from the bed.

Willie advanced on the bed, squinting. "That old man, Absalom, didn't disappear for nothing. And you ain't in that bed for nothing."

"I fell down in the woods," David said. "It can happen anywhere."

"But it happened there. And if somebody killed Dad, that means there may be somebody out there who doesn't *want* you or anybody else to find anything. I can't ask you to keep going if you might get killed.''

I looked at David and he gave a little nod.

"I understand your being worried," I said quietly. "But we aren't about to give up if you don't."

Willie stared me in the eye and then looked over at David.

"You don't think I'm a dumb coonass, like my dad?"

"Never thought that about either of you," I said.

Willie pounded his fist against his thigh. "Guys, you gotta find whatever it is. You gotta make sense of why my dad died."

"We'll do our best," I promised.

I guided him to the door and closed it behind him.

When I turned back to the bed I heard David exhale. "I hope he makes it home." He took another sip from his water glass and grimaced.

"If I'm gonna risk my ass for this, seems like you could bring me something to *drink*?"

"Soon as you're off painkillers," I promised.

He grunted. "Alan . . ."

"Yeah?"

"What if we don't find squat?"

"Oh, I think we'll find *something*," I said.

"How the hell can you promise that?"

And that was when I reached into my pocket and showed him the little brass trade bell.

ELEVEN

When I left David I drove back to the office and parked outside with my motor running, thinking. I hadn't mentioned the brass bell to Willie because I didn't want to create false hope. It's one thing to find a few artifacts and another to find a whole cemetery. Besides, I'd seen projects where the archaeologist had to perform with his client looking over his shoulder and it doesn't work for anybody, believe me.

So I checked in at the office, was relieved there were no calls, and made a call of my own. Then I walked across the street to the university, a map cylinder under my arm.

The Italianate buildings, sand-colored with tile roofs, fronted a parade ground, where the cadet corps marched twice a week. In the seventy years since the campus had moved here from the old location downtown, it had come to fill an area of about six hundred acres, and many of the grassy vistas I remembered from childhood had become parking lots.

By the time I reached the shade on the far side of the parade ground I was soaked as well as parched. I sucked in the cool air of the geology building and took the elevator to the third floor. I passed under an emblem that said LOUISIANA, GEOLOGICAL SURVEY, 1934, and down a hallway. Lars Kjelgard had his office door half-open when I stopped outside.

"Alan, come in and tell me what brings you to calling me after you don't come up here in so long," Lars cried, rising to give me a two-handed shake. A solidly built man in his late thirties, Lars had longish, prematurely gray hair, and a way of killing the king's English when he spoke.

"A question," I said. "The kind I only trust you to answer."

"Somebody trusts me?" Lars snorted. "You know I'm on the Corps of Engineers shit book after I told them they can't put that canal north of the city without they run into sand before they got the bore holes drilled good." He made a face of mock pain. "They say I made them all kinds of embarrassment."

"I bet you did."

"So what is it now?" he demanded. "They sent you to offer me money to recant?"

"Not exactly." I laughed. "It's just a little problem of alluvial geomorphology."

He nodded gravely. "We do that here," he said.

I took the topographic map out of the map tube and he made a place for it on his study table. Over the table, on the wall, was a framed certificate from some South Louisiana mayor, declaring Dr. Lars Kjelgard an honorary Cajun.

"You see this island?" I asked, indicating the strip where P. E. and I had ended up.

"Yah, I see it." He turned his head to give me a puzzled look.

"Any thoughts as to when it was formed?"

"Yah, I got thoughts on that." He squinted at me. "But why you want to know?"

"Just a project I'm doing," I said. "I need to know if the place is worth checking for sites earlier than, say, the middle of the last century."

Lars sighed. "This island is part of an old river meander. I think if you check your Mississippi River Commission maps from the last century you see that until 1886, the river was right against the hills there. Then it meandered west after that, during the flood of '87. That left this area exposed."

He pulled out some blue-line maps and put them on the table, over my topographic sheet. I'd seen the maps before.

They were issued by the Mississippi River Commission on a periodic basis, and I'd meant to check them before we went to the field again.

I watched him compare two of the maps and saw that what he was saying was true: The island and the floodplain leading to the island had been part of the river until 1887.

"Well," I said, looking up. "I'm impressed."

"Yah, it's kinda like I read your mind, yah?"

"Kind of."

"Like I see you coming, I know from the map tube you got a project, but the right half your face is sunburned, so I know you been facing north in the afternoon. Now, from the scratches on your arms, I know you're in briars, but the kind of scratches only match the kind that grows in a certain place in West Feliciana Parish. So, putting three and two together . . ."

"How did you know, Lars?"

He shrugged. "Because somebody else was in here right before, asking the same questions. That's how I got the commission maps right here still: I was going over it with her."

"Her?"

"Yah, pretty girl she was, too, and not married. I look for the fingers, you know, to see rings. None."

I took a deep breath. "This girl . . ."

But Lars was fumbling in his desk drawer.

"She give me a card. Here."

I didn't have to look at it, because I already knew what it would say:

Courtney & Associates.

It took me ten minutes to make my way back through the body-melting heat so that by the time I got to my car it was just after four. I'd need another quarter of an hour to reach her office and I didn't know if she'd still be there.

I was too irked not to try.

I took the road between the lakes, with the raised freeway on my left, and caught Perkins Road just before Stanford. On the maps of the last century, the road was shown as a track to Dr. Perkins's Plantation. Today it's a clogged artery leading east, from the outskirts of the Garden District to the new suburbs on the city's eastern edge. About a mile along, on the right, in some land I remembered as woods when I was a little boy, an enterprising developer had built a small park of gray, wooden buildings that housed suites of offices. According to the sign, there was a home improvement service, an insurance office, and a clinical psychologist. I didn't see any shingle for Courtney & Associates, but then I reminded myself that she was new. If she stayed more than a month she'd probably get around to it.

As I pulled into the parking lot I glimpsed the white Integra a few doors down. I stopped next to it and saw that Suite 107 was the door in front of me. I took a deep breath and pushed it open.

I found myself in a carpeted room with a front desk and a couple of plastic basket chairs. The paintings on the wall were generic rivers and mountains—only a step up from black felt Elvis. There was no one at the desk and no sign that anyone had ever worked there. To the left of the desk a door led into the rear of the complex.

"Hello," I said. "Is anybody here?"

I heard a shuffling from somewhere in the rear, then steps padding toward me.

"Who is it?" She materialized in the doorway, a manila folder in her hand, and froze as she saw me.

"Oh. It's you."

"Who did you think it was?" I asked acidly. "The world beating a path to your door?"

"No, I thought it was the insurance salesman down the way," she said coolly. "He keeps finding excuses to come in and *orientate* me."

"And you don't like him."

"I don't like the word *orientate*. And I don't like being slobbered over by married men."

"I'd think you were safe," I said and got a withering look in return.

"So what do you want?" she demanded, folding her arms.

"I want to know why you went to Lars Kjelgard," I said.

She stared at me for a second, as if trying to decide whether to retreat or brazen it out. Finally she shrugged.

"I was curious about the landform," she said. "I was wondering if there could possibly be anything old on that island or whether it would have to be recent."

"I see. You don't understand yet that this isn't your project?"

"It seems to me that almost getting killed out there gives me some rights," she said.

"Our workers' comp and general liability cover accidents to our people. When somebody else invites themselves along, it throws our legal situation into a cocked hat."

P. E. Courtney shook her head slowly and tsked.

"I would have thought you could do better than trot out insurance technicalities. You sound like a lawyer, not an archaeologist."

I folded my arms.

"Speaking of that, where are these famous *associates* that you've got on your business card? All I see here is a rental office with a nameplate on the door. Where's your lab? Where's your equipment? And don't reach for your pack. I mean your *real* equipment, like your flotation tank, your water screens, your magnetometer?"

Her lips pursed. "I can get all those things," she said tightly. "But that isn't all there is to archaeology. Without theory, without knowing what paradigm you're trying to falsify, you're just an antiquarian."

"Paradigm? Falsify? If you'd been out of graduate school long enough to get rid of that gobbledygook they foist on you, you'd know none of it's worth Confederate money without fieldwork, without knowing how to handle yourself in the woods, to—"

She pinioned me with her eyes. "I seem to have handled myself well enough today," she said quietly.

She had me there.

"Look," I said, carefully changing the subject. "You'll probably do very well down here. I'm just saying you need some tempering, so to speak—some real fieldwork.''

She nodded, turned suddenly, and started for the back. ''Come back,'' she said in a voice almost too low to hear. Curious, I followed.

''Since you're here, I'd like to get your opinion of something,'' she said.

I stared, nonplussed. ''Sure,'' I said finally.

I followed her down the hallway to her private office, on the right. Once inside, I saw a big poster of the sarcophagus lid from the tomb of Pacal at Palenque. On the other wall was a framed photo of an excavation in progress, the earth neatly staked off into squares and people bent over in the half-excavated units. And below this photograph was a small bookshelf, within easy reach of the Formica desk. She took a volume from the shelf. I saw that it was one of the Peabody Museum reports, from Harvard.

''What do you think of this?'' she asked.

I turned the work over in my hands.

Excavations at the Polhugh Site, Kentucky (1992–1994), the title said.

''I think everybody holds Paul Oldham in high regard,'' I said, referring to the author. ''I don't know him well, but he does damn fine work. Why? Did you work with him?''

''You might say that,'' she said dryly. ''I wrote the book.''

''You what?''

She nodded at the book I was holding. ''I wrote it. I also ran the field crew. If you look at the acknowledgments, you'll see my name.''

I turned to the first part of the book, which listed the people who had participated in the project.

The author especially wishes to thank Miss P. E. Courtney, who ably supervised field operations and contributed both to the analysis and to the writing of the final report.

''I don't understand,'' I said.

''No? It's easy. Paul Oldham told me I could have this as a doctoral project. He got the funds and then came down maybe twice the whole time to visit the excavation. I did most of the analysis and wrote the manuscript, but when I saw the finished product it had his name on it. I was just the *field supervisor*."

"Christ."

She shrugged. "It happens all the time, professors stealing their students' work. Only this was worse than most, because he was drinking himself into retirement after his wife died and all the other faculty wanted to ease him out without a big flap. So they asked me to go easy, not say anything, and one of them helped me change my dissertation to ceramic analysis, using the same data and bringing in some data from a few other sites."

I thought of all the times I'd seen Paul Oldham at meetings, giving papers to hushed and admiring audiences. Once I'd even been in the same bar with him, listened to his anecdotes about fieldwork.

I frowned. "But I thought your dissertation had to do with contact period sites in the Yazoo Basin."

"My M.A. thesis," she corrected.

Leave it to Freddie St. Ambrose to get it all wrong, I thought.

"So now you're pissed at Harvard," I said.

"Some people there," she agreed. "But that's not why I'm here. I'm down here for the reasons I told you, and some personal ones."

I started to say something, but I had a feeling she wasn't about to open up any further.

"Okay," I said, keeping my voice low. "But it's still going to take more than a rented suite. You've got to understand: You can't just show up one day and expect to get a slice of things. It's nothing personal—"

"Isn't it?"

"No. I mean, what . . . ?"

"You Southerners don't much like independent women," she said. "Well, I knew it would take some effort to crash the good old boy network. I'm willing to take a few knocks. But don't expect me not to knock back."

"Knock back? Seems to me all you've been doing is knocking, ever since you've been down here. You act like the world is going to open up and welcome you. Well, the profession we're in isn't glamorous, like being a university archaeologist. No slide shows to impress students. We make our living from clients that mostly consider us a nuisance. They don't give a damn if you've got an office in Doctor's Plaza, or if you dress like Panama Jack . . .''

I saw her stiffen and knew I scored. "Most of 'em wish they didn't have to fool with us at all, because we're just part of a federal permitting process they see as a burden. But if they *have* to deal with us, they want only a few things: They want us to be cheap, they want us to be fast, and they want us to make the bureaucrats who review their applications happy. Most of our clients would level the Great Pyramid if they wanted to build a shopping mall there. So we go out and bake our brains in the sun and stumble through briar patches and when we come out some desk jockey at the Corps of Engineers wants to know if we did a shovel test in a place where there's three feet of water, or they want to know why we didn't use a screen when we're in solid clay. Nobody's ever retired from this field, because it's too new, but a lot have dropped out along the way, or given up in disgust, or just plain gone bankrupt.''

She stared at me for a long time, and I wasn't sure what effect my lecture had had. Then she said quietly:

"I don't intend to fail. I *can't* fail." For an instant I saw her without the veneer of self-confidence, almost, well, *vulnerable.*

"As for Panama Jack—" she began, but I cut her off.

"I take it back." I looked at the photograph on her wall and realized that one of the diggers in the picture was the woman in the room with me, three or four years younger, perhaps, and with dirt on her face. "But you have to realize it doesn't go over so well when somebody starts trying to appropriate somebody else's project.''

"I told you, I'm not trying to appropriate anything. I was just doing research." She put her hands on her hips. "I was trying to help.''

I shook my head, not sure if any of this was getting through. "If you'd called me first . . .''

And to my surprise, she nodded. "Yes. You're right. I should have. I got carried away." Her turn to shrug. "It's always been a problem with me: too much enthusiasm.''

"Well, it's better than not giving a damn, I guess."

I turned around and started out. I'd gotten midway through the front office when she called after me:

"What now?"

"I dunno. Play it by ear, I guess." I turned partway round to face her. "Look, I'll give you a call."

"Sure," she said. "Look, if this is a kiss-off, I'd rather you just said it."

"It's not a kiss-off," I said. "I just have to think."

She nodded, unconvinced. "I'll be here," she said. "But I want you to get one thing straight."

"Yeah?"

"I've never gotten my field clothes from Panama Jack."

TWELVE

I woke up late Wednesday morning. When I looked in the mirror I saw scratches on my arms and face, and hollows under my eyes. I was getting too old for this work, but I wasn't sure what happened to old contract archaeologists. Maybe, I thought, they got catalogued and stuck away on some museum shelf. More likely they just died in the woods and were left for the carrion eaters. Or . . . Digger poked with a cold snout, telling me to stop indulging myself when he still hadn't been fed.

"It's easy for you," I said, remembering the times I'd taken him out to the country and he'd bounded straight for the worst thicket.

I checked in at the office and was happy to find there was no crisis and that Willie's check had been honored, allowing us to make payroll. With the pressure lifted for another pay cycle, I drove to the hospital, where the nurse told me David was about to go home. I congratulated him and promised to call later. Then I drove up to St. Francisville.

I wasn't sure what I was looking for, but it's good procedure to check conveyance records when you're surveying a piece of land. Conveyance records can strip away today's smiles and reveal old feuds, lawsuits, and bankruptcies. Maybe there was somebody who had an emotional claim to the place. Somebody willing to kill T-Joe to validate that claim.

The courthouse is a cool, stately old structure built in the first days of the century, when wagons creaked through the dirt streets. Oak trees shade the lawn and there are the obligatory memorials to lost causes. Inside, I went directly to the Clerk of Court's office and was shown the conveyance books.

There was nothing very mysterious about the Dupont parcel, though. It had been purchased nine months before, from Carter Wascom Jr., just as Willie said. The price was $1.25 million and the description was the usual:

> *Twelve hundred acres in Sections 10 and 11, Township 12 North, Range 3 East, being that land bounded on the north by State Highway 24 and on the east by Greenbriar Plantation, and on south by the course of a certain bayou and on the west by the left descending bank of the Mississippi River, with the exception of four acres fronting on Highway 24, owned by Marcus Briney, and three and one half acres on Highway 24, and adjacent to the aforesaid Briney property on the north, owned by Carter Wascom Jr.*

I stared at the record for a moment, considering the implications: Absalom Moon didn't own his property; he was a tenant of Carter Wascom.

Then I looked up Briney and found that his own plot, consisting of ten acres, had been purchased from Carter and Eulalia Wascom in 1992, for the sum of five thousand dollars.

So when Eulalia had become sick, and there were bills to pay, Carter had sold a small amount of land to Briney but Absalom Moon hadn't had the money or the credit to buy his own land. Much later, T-Joe Dupont had acquired twelve hundred acres, but there'd been another major selloff before him. I checked under Wascom's name, in the vendor list, and there it was:

> *Fourteen hundred acres sold by Carter Wascom Jr. to the local utilities company in 1978. Price, $1.4 million.*

Then, eighteen years later, Wascom had been forced to sell more land.

Where had the $1.4 million gone?

I followed the property back to the last century, to see if there were others associated with the plantation. The Wascoms, however, had owned it since just after the Civil War, when Lucas Wascom had purchased it at a sheriff's sale from Marie Clayton, the widow of the former owner who had apparently died during the war. Chester Clayton, her husband, had bought it in 1830, from one Juan Villareal, who, according to the faded notation, had received it from the Spanish crown when West Florida was a Spanish possession. I wondered idly if the Wascoms were locals or carpetbaggers from the North who'd pounced on an opportunity. I checked the name in the index and found other Wascoms, so they must have lived hereabouts. Still, I thought, it couldn't have made them popular, evicting a widow lady. But maybe, on the other hand, they had done her a favor. It was a common enough situation after the war. In any case, it was unlikely anyone around today knew or much cared.

I left the courthouse, with the feeling of having left something undone. Something rubbed on me like a pebble in my shoe, but I couldn't place it. I stood on the sidewalk, watching the cars creep past. Across the street, behind an iron fence, was the old Episcopalian cemetery, where the gentry of the last century were buried. On impulse, I walked over and made my way through the graves. The two Feliciana Parishes, West and East, were settled primarily by Anglos, during the brief British ownership of West Florida. When the Spanish had taken over in 1783, the Anglo settlers had at first accepted the change, but later had grown restless. By 1810, after the territory to the west and south had been accepted into the Union through the Louisiana Purchase, they had mounted a brief rebellion against the Spanish, with the result that after a few weeks the West Florida Republic, as they'd called it, also became a part of the United States. Many of these original settlers were buried in this cemetery, and I had in my mind that I might run across the Wascom plot.

Instead, I ran into Carter Wascom himself.

He was standing off in a corner, near the grill fence, partly shielded by a gray marble obelisk. As I watched, he stooped and appeared to lay something on the ground. I ducked back out of sight and watched as he strode quickly from the graveyard, shoulders hunched. When he was gone I walked over to where he'd stood and looked down.

The graves were those of the Wascom family, as I'd suspected, beginning with *Lucas Wascom, Esq.*, whose obelisk marked the plot. The *Esq.* made it plain enough: He'd been a lawyer, probably drawing up deeds and conveyances and then buying up what fell his way.

At the bottom of the obelisk were the names of his wife, Rebecca, and three of the children. Their graves, complete with head markers and foot stones, stretched at the base of the stela. Beside the first Wascoms, later generations of the family filled the rest of the plot, until there, in one corner, was a newer, standing memorial, seemingly out of place. On it were the names of Carter and Eulalia Wascom.

Below her name were her dates (January 5, 1943—June 11, 1993) and the inscription,

> *Underneath this stone doth lie*
> *As much beauty as could die;*
> *Which in life did harbor give*
> *to more virtue than doth live.*

I scribbled down the lines, and looked over at Carter Wascom's inscription. After his birth date (November 15, 1934) was a single line of Latin:

> *Fiat justitia, ruat caelum.*

I copied this, too, and then stared at the wreath on the grave. A sudden chill came over me when I realized that this was the fourth anniversary of her death.

THIRTEEN

I drove south to the nuclear plant and showed my driver's license at the front gate. I told the guard I'd come to see Aaron Chustz. The guard nodded and checked a list, then called ahead. He told me Mr. Chustz was in his office.

Ten years ago, before Sam MacGregor had retired, he and I had done a project for the utilities company, here on the grounds. They'd found part of an old sugar mill and we'd had to evaluate it for historical value. We'd spent a couple of cold winter days digging up bricks and had warmed ourselves afterward around the fire at Aaron's place. The sugar mill had turned out not to be that important, and it had pertained to the plantation adjacent to Greenbriar, so I hadn't made Carter Wascom's acquaintance then. But somehow I had the feeling it might have saved time if I had.

I parked in front of the one story administration building and showed my pass to the guard inside. But he'd hardly had a chance to examine it before Aaron appeared, smiling. In ten years his dark hair had receded to the middle of his head and he was wearing horn-rims I didn't remember, but he had the same grin and the same friendly handshake. He waited while I signed in and then led me down the corridor to his office.

"How's Dr. MacGregor?" he asked. "I'll never forget those stories he used to tell."

I told him Sam was fine, thriving in retirement in his big

house in Iberville Parish, downriver from Baton Rouge. "I still see him every few months," I said.

Aaron closed the door behind him, indicated a padded chair, and took a seat behind his desk.

"So what can I do for you?" he asked, leaning back in his chair.

"Aaron, you're still the justice of the peace for this parish, aren't you?" I asked.

He nodded, his smile fading. "That's right. Is there a problem?" Then his smile flashed back: "Or did you come up here about a wedding?"

"No wedding," I said. "And no problem I can put my finger on. But, to be honest, Aaron, I figured that since you work here at the plant as well as being the JP for this parish, you'd be the one with the best information."

"Well," he allowed, tugging an ear, "I do perform a lot of weddings and I even write out a few arrest warrants, if that's what you mean. And I do hear quite a bit, on all sides. But what was it particularly?"

I told him about T-Joe's death and how David had been injured, and also about the odd way in which P. E. and I had been pursued, holding back only the part about finding the little brass bell.

"To be honest," I concluded, "I was curious about your neighbor, Carter Wascom."

Aaron nodded then, as if it all made sense. "Carter, eh? I see what you're getting at. Carter Wascom's a mighty strange bird. Of course, whether he's *that* strange, to follow folks into the woods and try to scare 'em, I couldn't say. But he's definitely what the surveyors call half a bubble off."

"I understand his wife's death was what did it to him," I said.

Aaron took a deep breath.

"Well, it hit him hard, that's true. But, you know, Carter never was quite what you'd call normal. Even when he was little he was different. Kept to himself, wrote poems, stayed inside. Was raised by his mother and a couple of old aunts. His father drowned in some kind of accident right after he was born. I think people were pretty surprised he got married at all. Then, when it turned out to be his cousin—''

''His cousin?''

''Third, I think she was. Just inside the legal limits. Story is she came to visit one day, when she was just a girl, and he decided he had to have her. Well''—he gestured—''that's the way Carter is: Gets a notion in his head and you can't budge him.''

''The relatives didn't mind?''

''The girl was from a poorer branch of the family, and Carter was worth a good bit, with Greenbriar and all. All they did was make a condition: Carter would have to wait until she was twenty-one. That meant waiting eight years.''

''You mean she was only thirteen when they met?''

''That's right. And I think their thought was he'd probably forget, or else she'd find somebody else, but Carter was never one to be moved by anybody else's logic. He waited 'em out and on her twenty-first birthday he claimed his right to ask her to marry him and she accepted, so what could they do?''

I was trying to visualize the young Carter Wascom, in the big house, surrounded by elderly women.

''How did she fit in with all the aunts and the mother?'' I asked.

Aaron gave a little chuckle.

''You'd think she'd've had the odds against her, wouldn't you? But Eulalia was different. She wasn't scared of anybody or *anything*. Before you knew it, she had those old women buffaloed. I don't know how she did it. I'm not sure I *want* to know.''

''She must have been something special,'' I said.

''She was that, all right. She held her own against the old women in the house. Then, about ten years after they married, when the older ladies were all gone, she really came out.''

He shook his head, remembering. ''Parties, trips, always entertaining people. You'd have thought she'd turned Carter inside out. He wasn't the same man. And I don't think that house had seen so much going on since the Civil War. You wouldn't believe some of the things she put on there: A Christmas party with all the women in these Civil War dresses, with the big skirts, a twenty-piece band, the men in Confederate uniforms . . . And Eulalia, naturally, was dressed up like Scarlett O'Hara. She even had Carter done up like Rhett Butler, poor bastard.'' He raised both hands. ''It must have cost 'em thousands of dollars. And it was going on all the time.''

I tried to visualize the old house as it must have been ten years ago, every window blazing, the lawn sprinkled with lights, couples dancing on the perfectly manicured lawn . . .

''Does Carter have a profession?'' I asked.

''Carter?'' Aaron guffawed. ''Carter was trained to be a *gentleman*. His mother taught him it wasn't good manners to work. And she always told him he was too sickly, anyway. Naw, Carter was rich enough to live off his inheritance.''

''But it didn't last, did it?''

''No way. Not with Eulalia. Not with trips to Europe every year, and safaris to Africa, and tours to South America. Not to mention some sizable donations to charity.''

''Eulalia is why he had to sell off a part of Greenbriar, then,'' I suggested.

Aaron nodded emphatically. ''Absolutely. She was spending them to the poorhouse. I know for a fact he didn't want to let it go. I notarized the sale, and he wasn't a happy camper. But he couldn't turn her down. Anything Eulalia wanted, she got.''

''I guess they went through the money from the sale then,'' I said.

Aaron nodded again. ''That's what they did. Percy Kling was the family lawyer. He went to see Carter three or four times to try to warn him, but Carter was like a man under a spell. Then something happened, I don't know what, because Percy wouldn't ever talk about it. But he washed his hands of the whole business. We knew then there couldn't be any good outcome. Carter even had a row with his folks, in Natchez. I heard they cut him off.''

I felt a sinking feeling, as though I were there to witness the debacle, and it was all unfolding in front of my eyes.

For a long time there was silence and I knew Aaron was

also in the past, reliving it all. Finally I heard him sigh.

"Then Eulalia got sick."

Something stabbed me like a knife, as if I were hearing the news about someone I really knew.

"At first she treated it like it didn't exist. That's the tragedy, you know? Eulalia was living in a magic world where things always went her way. If she'd just come down once to the real world, gone to a doctor, she'd be alive today. Instead . . ."

He picked up a little crystal paperweight and held it up to the light, staring at one of the facets.

"Naturally, he took her to the best clinics in this country and Europe, and when they couldn't do any good he paid for some expensive quack cure. It didn't do any good, either."

Another silence.

"I hear he holds the nuclear plant responsible."

Aaron nodded sadly. "Well, it couldn't have been just some little gene that went bad, could it? It had to be something Carter could point his finger at and hate. And we were there. We were the ones who took half his property. Paid him top dollar, but he kind of forgot that in his grief. The way he saw it, it must have been something we did, some chemical, some radioactivity in the water or the air."

"I understand there've been some lawsuits."

"One, and he lost. There simply wasn't any proof. But Carter won't give up. You see"—Aaron leaned toward me, his face drawn —"Carter doesn't have anything else to live for."

I shifted my chair, as a way to break the spell.

"It's a sad business," Aaron said, voicing my thoughts. "But, look, you don't really think Carter's the one who was chasing you in the woods?"

"I can't see any reason why he would, but somebody did. How does he get along with his neighbors, by the way?"

"You mean Briney and old Absalom?" Aaron shrugged. "All right, I guess. I know he didn't want to sell that lot Marcus bought, but he needed the money. As for Absalom, well, he's been living there forever. For all I know, the

Moons were slaves on the old place during the War.''

"Isn't it strange Briney decided to live down here, at the southern end of the parish instead of up near the prison, where most of the people who work there live?"

"Not really. See, Marcus used to live in one of the houses on the prison grounds. Then the administration changed and they decided the people who lived in state-owned houses would have to start paying rent, so Marcus took retirement and made Carter an offer on his little piece of land."

"At five grand, he only paid half what it was worth, if the other sales are an indication."

"Carter's no businessman," Aaron said. "He'd have some money left if he was."

I got up slowly, feeling as if I'd lived through a hundred years of history. Suddenly I remembered what had been bothering me when I'd left the Clerk of Court's office. "You mentioned that Eulalia was Carter Wascom's third cousin."

Aaron Chustz nodded.

"Isn't Warden Goodeau a cousin, too?"

"That's right. Carter's mother and Levi's mother were sisters."

I opened the door. "I appreciate your filling me in, Aaron. By the way, I don't guess I'd get anywhere talking to this lawyer, Percy Kling?"

"Nowhere at all," Aaron said. "Percy died last year. But look, you aren't planning to go poking around some more down there until this is figured out, are you?"

"Well, not until they catch those escapees, anyway," I said.

Aaron stared back at me, wooden-faced: "You won't have to worry about them. I talked to the sheriff yesterday: They tried to swim the river."

"You mean . . ."

He nodded. "They both drowned."

▰▰▰Fourteen

I left the administration building and headed back to the main highway. As I waited at the blinking light for the traffic to pass I kept thinking about T-Joe. Was I any closer to an answer about his death? Or to learning why Absalom had vanished into the woods?

There was one more card I had to play. When the last car had passed, I turned left, toward St. Francisville, instead of right, toward Baton Rouge.

Once more I turned off the highway and into the center of town, but this time I went past the courthouse and all the way to the end of the shady street, to where the pavement ended. Before me was the river, and at the bottom of the slope a couple of cars waited, as well as a bicyclist and a man selling roasted peanuts. The air smelled of mud and oil and my tires crackled on the gravel as I rolled downhill toward the water's edge.

Midway out, and half a mile away, the ferry appeared to float helplessly, like a cloud, but I knew its powerful diesels were in reality pushing it toward us, against the current. Fifteen minutes later, standing at the rail and feeling the hot wind in my face, I felt sorry for the two men who had given themselves to the river, rather than face human justice. Their bodies were probably almost to Baton Rouge now. It was a thought I found too chilling to hold for long, the idea of those churning depths, and I turned away just in time to see the opposite shore looming before me.

I bypassed the tiny resort community of New Roads,

on the banks of an old river channel, and kept on up Highway 1.

Maybe I was wasting my time, but it was worth a try. That's what I told myself, anyway. Maybe I just didn't have a better option.

Carter Wascom needed money because his beloved Eulalia had spent him almost to the poorhouse. Even with her gone, he'd wasted thousands on a fruitless lawsuit. What if he'd found out somehow there was treasure buried in the ground nearby?

Except that the Tunica artifacts weren't treasure in the ordinary sense. He might realize ten or twenty thousand on the artifact market, but was he that desperate? Would he kill?

It was one-thirty when I reached the outskirts of Marksville, the seat of Avoyelles Parish. I realized I hadn't eaten, but decided lunch could wait. As I neared the Tunica Reservation, I saw the vast, low casino building that was supposed to make the tribe rich. Ironically, just ahead, on the same side of the highway, was a pyramid covered with kudzu grass. Inside the pyramid, in a special display area, was the original Tunica Treasure. The treasure brought by the white men, I thought, just like the treasure being shoved across the green felt at the roulette and craps tables.

I turned in and parked in front of the museum. In the background were houses that were indistinguishable from those HUD had built in a thousand other places in the country, all seemingly to the same plan and with the same lack of imagination.

As I got out I noticed a trio of young men standing in front of the low, functional-looking building that served as a community center and tribal headquarters. As I walked down the sidewalk toward the museum I felt their eyes on my back. I opened the big glass door and murmured a prayer of thanks for the air conditioning.

The woman at the reception counter, who had seen me coming up the walk, smiled.

"It's hot," she said, and I nodded. She had a broad, dark face and friendly eyes. I smelled the half-eaten hamburger on the counter in front of her and realized suddenly that I was hungry.

"Alan." I turned at the sound of my name. Frank LeMoine was standing in the doorway of the curator's office, his big frame filling the opening, a grin on his face. "What brings you up here?"

We shook hands and LeMoine eyed me critically.

"You haven't put on any meat," he said. "Don't you have somebody down there to feed you?"

I instinctively sucked in my stomach. "You make me feel good, Frank. You're looking good, too."

He patted his own generous paunch.

"I'm not on a hunger strike," he laughed. "I'll leave that to white men." He took my arm. "Come on, lemme introduce you to my assistant and show you the last display we put up."

We walked into the main display room, where a thin young man who couldn't have been more than eighteen was arranging items in a display case in the center.

"Dr. Alan Graham, this is Ben Picote. He's been working with me for the past couple of months."

The boy and I shook hands and he probed me with his dark eyes.

"You're an archaeologist," he said.

"That's right."

"Ben did a lot of this," Frank bragged, gesturing to the glass cases along the walls. Inside the cases I saw rusted muskets, faience and majolica vessels from Europe, and pots made by the Indians themselves with the traditional cross-hatched designs and looping swirls. And in one case was a display of beads and little brass bells.

"We got this lot cleaned up and put in the case just last week," Frank said. I stared down at a display of iron cooking pots of the kind the French had traded to the Tunica in the eighteenth century. With the arrival of the whites, the Tunica had become a nexus for trade, first as producers of salt, and later as horse traders, passing horses from the tribes to the west to the horse-poor French on the eastern side of the river. Payment for the horses had been guns, cooking ware, and decorative trinkets. The Tunica who had lived on Trudeau Plantation, below Angola, in the 1700s, had been rich indeed, and the items in the cases around me had come from their graves.

"Good job," I said. "Many visitors?"

"Plenty since the casino opened," Frank allowed. "Folks don't seem to be able to get enough of the slots."

"Cross your fingers," I said.

"Yeah." He laughed. "So what are you doing up this way?"

"Picking brains," I said. "You heard any rumors about the last Tunica village lately?"

Frank frowned. "You mean after they left Trudeau?" He shook his head. "No. Why, somebody think they found it?"

"I dunno. There're rumors."

The boy stepped forward. "We don't want anybody digging up any more of our ancestors."

"I know. I'm not talking about myself. I thought maybe somebody might have come around here, asking."

"They have. You."

"If the wrong person finds it, they'll dig it up, just like they did the first time," I said.

Frank LeMoine patted me on the shoulder and tried to laugh. "It's a sensitive subject, Alan. We haven't figured out yet who the wrong person is. Is it some Angola guard? Or an archaeologist?"

"You know no reputable archaeologist would risk his career breaking the law."

Ben Picote shook his head: "Is there such a thing as a reputable archaeologist?"

I'd touched a nerve and all I could do was back off.

"I'm not the enemy," I said quietly.

"Not Alan Graham, no," Frank said. "But what Ben's talking about is *Doctor* Alan Graham, and that could be something different."

"You have to make that judgment yourselves."

The curator cocked his head and put a hand under his chin, pretending to consider. "Hmmmm. White eyes speak with forked tongue—sometimes." He winked at his assistant. "I think we better feed up this one so when we eat him there'll be some flesh on his bones." He clapped me on the shoulder. "Come on, I'll take you to lunch."

"Thanks, Frank, but I've got to get back," I said.

He didn't argue, because we both realized the bonhomie had been shattered by the memory of events that stretched far beyond our own individual lives. As I left, I felt Ben's eyes on me, burning into my back.

FIFTEEN

I got back to town just in time to beat the afternoon rush and drove over to David's apartment. He hobbled to the door and smiled when he saw me. I realized Elizabeth hadn't returned from work yet and felt a flush of guilt at having disturbed him, but he seemed glad for the company. He flopped back into his easy chair and propped his leg on the footstool. I told him about my trip to the clerk's office, my conversation with Aaron Chustz, and then about my drive to Marksville.

"I couldn't think of anything else to do," I said lamely. "I guess I was hoping something would jump out at me, but it didn't."

"They never found old Absalom?" he asked.

"Nobody seems very concerned. I get the feeling he's done this before."

"And the competition?" It took a few seconds before I realized he was talking about P. E. Courtney.

"Haven't heard from her," I said.

"Archaeobitches," he sneered. "Why do we have to be surrounded by them?"

I remembered the suddenly vulnerable look on P. E.'s face as we stood in her office and I gave a little shrug.

"I'm not sure she's so bad."

"That's what you said about Bombast, and then she canceled the scope of work for the Terrebonne project."

"There's that," I admitted grimly. "But to compare her to Bombast—"

"Be warned." He lifted a hand. "You're always giving people the benefit of the doubt, especially women. But take it from an old married man: You heard it here first."

I left him ensconced and went home with a sour feeling about everything. He was probably right: I *was* being too soft. P. E. Courtney had materialized from nowhere and tried, unabashedly, to steal our project. What did I owe her? Why did I even care what she thought? After all, she was competition, in a field where there was room for only so many competitors, and it was unfair for her to use her sex— I caught myself there. She *hadn't* used her sex, and maybe that was what bothered me, because I'd grown up in the South, where it was expected. Women were supposed to bat their eyes, coo, and flounce, but P. E. Courtney did none of these. So to me she came across as cold—except for the instant when I'd seen her with her defenses down.

I fed Digger and asked him afterward what he thought of her. He crawled into my lap, put his paws on either side of his nose, and gave me a sad look.

"What do you know?" I asked him. "You haven't even seen her."

I opened the refrigerator and saw more of the overcooked jambalaya from Saturday night. Time to throw it out, I told myself. But I wasn't in the mood to start another culinary project, so I pulled out some frozen tamales and then went back outside and stood on my sidewalk, watching the cars pass along the shady boulevard. I'd grown up here, spent years away, and then come back. I knew how it was to be in a strange place.

Oh, hell, there I went again. Soft, like David said.

Restless, I went to the Blazer and unlocked it. I slid behind the wheel, sat there a moment, and then made up my mind.

Sam. Sam would know what to make of it all, both of the attractive P. E. Courtney and of the strange business of the Tunica artifacts. And if he didn't know, I'd at least come away feeling better.

He lived on the River Road, about ten miles south of the university, in neighboring Iberville Parish. It was a rural setting, with the nearest house a half-mile away, and fifty acres of grazing land for cows and horses. In his second retirement, Sam now lived the life of a country squire, and once he told me he thought he was the reincarnation of the man who had owned the land during the Civil War, but that was only after a few rounds of J. W. Dant, which could make Sam say anything.

So why wasn't I headed down the River Road?

Because, I told myself, Sun Tzu said intelligence is the essence of winning wars. Or something like that. And if he'd had a P. E. Courtney on his case, he'd have made damn sure where she was before he took off.

She'd probably left her office two hours ago. There wasn't a thing for her to do there, anyway, but stare at the posters and polish her nails. That was *if* she polished her nails . . .

I turned into the lot and saw the white Integra, sitting there like a ghost in the gloaming. There was a light in her window. She hadn't left.

So I'd pinned her down. And that was when my plan materialized from the warm night air (As if it hadn't been in my unconscious all along!).

I'd take her to Sam and see what he thought. Eyeball to eyeball.

After all, he was the one who'd coined the term *archaeo-bitch*. How many times had I heard him rail about "damn women in archaeology"? The perfect sexist, seventy-five years old, and knowing he could say anything he damn pleased.

I'd bring him a bottle of Dant's, hundred proof, along with a not so fine P. E. Courtney.

I got out and went to the office door.

It was locked.

I knocked three times and then pounded twice. A voice from behind the wood asked who it was.

"Me," I told her. "Alan."

The handle turned and the door opened.

"Oh. I'm sorry. I always lock it when I'm here alone."

"It's okay. I came to ask if you wanted to go to a seminar."

"A seminar?" She frowned.

"Well, informal-like. In a friend's house." I played my trump: "You know Sam MacGregor?"

"Dr. Sam MacGregor, who dug at Poverty Point and who worked at Baytown and who—"

"That one," I said. "A good friend of mine. We hoist a few every now and then and—"

"Where is he?"

"At his house," I said, hoping it was true. After all, I hadn't bothered to call ahead, and for all I knew Sam and Libby were out of the country. "I have a standing invitation."

"He won't mind if you bring someone?"

"I've done it before."

"I'll get my bag and lock up."

Which was how I found myself on a lonely road at just after dark with P. E. Courtney, the Girl Most Likely to Succeed in a Man's World, and a bottle of Dant's I'd picked up at a K&B drugstore.

A few cyclists were still out, their flickering headlamps shimmering like fireflies in the new darkness. I was tired from all the driving and I rolled down the window, hoping the blast of air would wake me up. A hot wind slapped my face, and in it I caught a whiff of cows and hay.

"This is pretty rural," P. E. ventured and I nodded.

She pointed at the barely visible embankment on our right. "This levee goes all the way to New Orleans, I take it."

"All the way," I said. "They built it in bits and pieces during the last century, as the plantations sprang up along the River Road."

"They," she said.

I turned my head to face her.

"Pardon?"

"You said, 'They built it.' I'm sure what you meant was that the slaves built it."

"Slaves, convicts, whoever was available."

"Which was slaves, mainly, and some convicts. Yes. Another version of Wittfogel's Oriental Despotism."

"Well, I don't think the slaves wanted to drown, either."

"Didn't they?"

"Well, most of 'em didn't." Unless, I thought, Old Massa's daughter was like P. E. Courtney.

She started to reply but I was already slowing for the driveway ahead. I turned off the asphalt, through the brick pillars and onto the shell drive. Relief spread through me as my headlights picked out Sam's Mercury station wagon, parked beside Libby's Lincoln Town Car.

I stopped behind the Merc and shut off my engine. Silence settled over us and then I heard the crickets and, from what seemed far away, the sound of a radio or television.

"Well?" P. E. Courtney demanded.

I got out and saw a figure framed against the soft light from inside.

"Who is it?" It was Libby's voice, carrying an uncharacteristic quaver.

"It's Alan," I said. "I was just driving around and—" It sounded too lame even for me so I stopped in midsentence.

"Oh, Alan . . ." Libby came down the steps toward me, hands outstretched, expression serious. "I'm so glad to see you. I thought for a minute it was Dr. Sonnier."

"Who?"

"Sam's been feeling badly lately. I just can't get him out of bed. It started with the flu but then . . ." She looked around and realized there was someone else in the car.

P. E. opened her door.

"Mrs. MacGregor, I'm sorry . . ." she began, shooting me a reproachful look, but Libby waved dismissively.

"Don't be. Sam will be so glad to see you. I'm sure part of it's just being retired, not having people come by like they used to."

"But—" My protest was brushed away.

"Come in, come in. I don't think Dr. Sonnier's coming, anyway. I twisted his arm to make a house call and he gave me a bunch of gobbledygook. You'd think my own niece's husband . . ."

She extended a hand to my companion.

"Hello. I'm Libby MacGregor."

"This is Prunella Courtney," I said quickly. "She's a

new archaeologist. I was trying to orient her."

P. E. started to say something, then wisely clamped her jaw shut.

We followed Libby into the house. The door had just closed when a voice rumbled down from somewhere above.

"Lib? Is that the goddamn doctor? I told you I didn't want to see him."

The little woman turned her face up to the stairs. "No, dear, it's Alan and a lady friend."

P. E. reached into her bag and brought out her card case. My groan was drowned out by the bellow from above:

"I'll be right down."

I looked over at Libby. "Maybe we ought to go."

But Libby shook her head: "Alan, he's refused to leave his bed for the last week. This may be better for him than a trip to the Mayo Clinic."

Seconds later I heard a shuffling from the top of the stairs, then a cough and a muttered oath. In another five seconds a pair of slippered feet appeared, and then the bottom of a plaid robe. Hands grasped the banister and Libby went forward to help, but the hands left their supports and waved her away.

"I'm not dead yet."

Libby moved aside and Sam MacGregor stood at the bottom of the stairs, beaming at us.

"Better keep away," he said as I came forward to take his hand, "I've got the galloping consumption."

I shook his hand anyway. It felt clammy.

"Have you got fever?" I asked.

"Hell, no." He rubbed a hand across his white beard and then his eyes fixed on P. E.

"Well, please introduce me . . ."

She was about to thrust a card at him when I lurched against her and knocked them to the floor. Before she could bend down I'd picked them up for her.

"This," I said, turning back to Sam, "is Prun—"

"Pepper," she blurted out then, her face a brilliant red. "My name is Pepper Courtney. I'm an archaeologist, I just came down from Harvard, I'm setting up to work here, and I don't know Dr. Graham well, in fact, not at all, so . . ."

"Pepper," Sam murmured, reaching out to take her hand in both of his. "What a charming name. I'm so happy you came to see an old has-been like me."

"Well . . ." I smirked as she fumbled for words. *Pepper. Her name was Pepper.*

"Tell me, how did you ever get such a wonderful name?" Sam demanded, herding us toward the living room. "Your father's idea, I'll bet."

"Why, yes."

"I know he's a man I'd get along with." He shuffled toward his easy chair and fell into it with a sigh. "My God, am I dry. And I haven't come all the way from Baton Rouge!"

I handed over the bottle and he cocked his head toward his wife. "I'll take Dant and water. What will you good people have?"

"Sam . . ." Libby began.

"Three fingers," he instructed and turned back toward us as a defeated Libby disappeared into the kitchen. "Thank God you came," he said *sotto voce*. "She won't make a scene in front of company."

"So what does the doctor say?" I asked, assessing his pallor. "Are you taking your medicine?"

"What doctor? What medicine?" he shot back. "You think I need those quacks? They'll do for you faster than a poor little virus. Besides . . ." He drew his robe closer about him. "Pneumonia is the old man's friend. Hits quick and takes you in a couple of days."

"No," Pepper breathed.

"Oh, for Christ's sake," I said. "You *haven't* been to the doctor?"

"What did I say? And that woman hid all my whiskey."

On cue, *that woman* returned then with three glasses on a tray. She served us and then turned stiffly toward Sam.

"Thank you, my dear." He whisked his glass off like a conjurer and held it up critically to the light. "Ummmm. A little on the light side, but . . . Will you join us, dearest?"

Libby gave him a strained smile and took a seat across the room. I saw Pepper glancing around her, at the shelves full of books on archaeology, history, and ancient languages.

"Well, cheers." Sam raised his glass and drained half of it. "Ahhh. I'm feeling better already."

Libby folded her arms. I knew she wasn't really angry; it was a little game they played, one they were both good at.

"Now . . ." Sam turned toward P. E., whom I was having trouble visualizing by her given name. "Tell me, Pepper, what brings you down here? You're in graduate school or you've completed it?"

"I got my doctorate last year," she explained in a subdued voice. "I came here because—"

Sam's eyes sparkled. "Did you study under Paul Oldham, by any chance?"

I watched her squirm. "He was my major professor when I started," she said. "But—"

"Incredible archaeologist," Sam began, cutting her off again. "I worked with him in Tennessee, in the late forties, you know. A fanatic for details. He had a mind like a trap. He could remember all kinds of things. And his interpretation of the Walters site was outstanding."

I noticed he was giving her a hard stare and she dropped her eyes.

"Of course you've read that report," he said genially.

"Yes." She reached for her drink in desperation.

"Paul and I had some times," Sam maundered. "Those were the days." He leaned toward her: "Not many women in archaeology back then. Florence Hawley, a handful of others. It was a man's world."

I watched to see if she'd bite but she mercifully kept her mouth shut.

" 'Course, not all the men were up to the job," Sam reminisced. "Hard business, being in the field so much. Some wives got tired and ran away. And some men got tired of their wives . . ." He chuckled. "A girl in every lab, if you know what I mean."

Pepper Courtney put her glass down hard on the coffee table.

"Paul Oldham wasn't one of those, though," Sam

drawled, taking another sip. He smacked his lips and held his glass out toward Libby. "Another drop or two, pet, eh? Less water this time, please?"

Libby pulled herself up and addressed us:

"Can I get a refill for you two?"

"Not yet," I said and Pepper shook her head. Sam handed his glass to Libby.

"Yes, Paul loved his wife. It was a hell of a thing the way she died." He shook his head. "Just withered away. Lou Gehrig's disease. Some linger for years, others go in a year or two. It took her seven years. It was no wonder the poor man starting drinking too much."

Libby returned and handed him his drink. He murmured thanks and sighed with pleasure as he tasted it.

"Better. A whole lot better, dear. Did you know Phyllis Oldham, Pepper?"

She shook her head quickly. "No."

"Beautiful woman. He was so dependent on her. Well . . . It was all tragic." He set his glass down and got up. I thought some of his usual color was back and he moved with more energy than when we'd first seen him. He strode over to the bookcase for one of the volumes and I realized with a surprise that it was the Peabody monograph on the Polhugh site.

"He sent this to me." Sam weighed the book in his hand and I watched Pepper redden. "Has an inscription and all. Let's see here, what did he say?" He opened the cover and leafed through the first few pages. "Oh, yes. *To my friend Sam MacGregor with best wishes, Paul Oldham.*" He handed the book to Pepper, who looked frantically for a way to avoid taking it, failed, and accepted it like a hot brick from the oven. Suddenly he was handing her a pen as well.

"I wonder, my dear, would you be kind enough to enter another inscription? Whatever you like, but just spell my name right." He cackled. "And add *from the author*. I think that'll give it more value."

I watched her mouth fall open.

"You . . . all along . . ."

"I *do* try to read the literature of my profession," Sam

said modestly, "and ever since I took a one-year visiting appointment at Harvard twenty years ago, I've more or less kept up with the scuttlebutt."

Slick, I thought, *very slick . . .*

"Of course, I didn't need scuttlebutt to tell me Paul hadn't done that report. The statistics were beyond him." He shrugged. "I've never seen a better analysis. I'm not running Paul down, of course: He was from the old school, before they taught archaeologists statistics. Why, I can't remember but one dissertation from our era that had any statistical analysis at all."

"I know," Pepper said quietly. "That was a comparative analysis of cervidae bones from twenty sites in the Southeast. *You* did it."

It was Sam's turn to look surprised.

"Alan, this young lady's a real prize. By God, she's right, too. It *was* a milestone, if I can blow my own horn. But so was hers."

Pepper was glowing now and I wanted to interrupt the love fest and tell him to cut the shit, but I knew better.

"I thought the multivariate analysis brought out some interesting correlations," she said primly. "The wear patterns on the chert knives suggested heavy usage as flaying implements used in the preparation of game."

"Considering all the deer bones around them," I said. "I'd have thought that was obvious."

"It was obvious the speed of light depended on the speed of the object from which it was emitted," she shot back. "Until Einstein, that is."

My turn to arch my brows. "Ever hear about the statistician who drowned in the creek with the average depth of three feet?" I asked blandly.

A gleeful Sam rubbed his hands together.

"Wonderful. I haven't had this much fun since I attended my last doctoral defense."

I looked over at Pepper: The woman was laughing.

"Oh, Dr. MacGregor . . ."

"Sam, please . . ."

I cleared my throat. "Well, we were just passing. I don't

want to tire you too much." I set my nearly empty glass on the tray.

"Don't go," Libby begged. "Sam's having fun. If you leave I'll have to listen to him moaning and complaining again."

"Me, complain?" Sam demanded. "Who lived a whole summer in a tent in the heat of the Louisiana rain forest? Who spent months as a castaway on a Caribbean island?"

"On your sabbatical," Libby said quietly. "On an island with seventy-two rum distilleries."

"It was an anthropological investigation."

Pepper spoke then:

"Tell us, Sam, what do you know about the last Tunica village on the east bank of the Mississippi? There's a rumor it's been rediscovered."

Sam stroked his white beard. "I've heard those stories. Once, Stu Neitzel and I even went beating around up there trying to find it, but we didn't have any luck. We finally figured it'd fallen in the river."

"We think so, too," I said quickly. "We're doing a survey on some land over on the east bank, just south of St. Francisville. I doubt there's anything there that's *in situ*."

"But, you know," Sam suggested, "we could all be wrong. Hell, archaeologists make a habit of being wrong. Sometimes I think we're lucky when things turn out *right*. We start with little fragments of pottery and pieces of bone and we try to make whole cultures come alive again. That's asking a hell of a lot." He held up his now empty glass, evinced surprise, and thrust it in Libby's direction. His long-suffering wife came forward to whisk it away to the kitchen.

"You watch," Sam whispered. "There won't be enough whiskey in there to taste. By the fourth drink I usually end up with tap water."

"When you get better," P. E. offered, "you'll have to come out with us."

Sam's face lit up. "I wouldn't miss it. Alan can make a gumbo. Did you know he's quite an accomplished chef? He did a whole *cochon d'lait* out here once for the annual Christmas party."

"Really," Pepper said, arching her brows at me. "I didn't know."

Sam cackled again: "Alan, have you been holding out on Pepper?"

"Right," I said woodenly.

Libby returned with a glass of what appeared, indeed, to be water. Sam held it to the light, sneered, and set it down on the tray. "There's probably a fish in it," he mumbled.

"But Alan's right," his new friend commented. "We really ought to leave. We've scheduled some fieldwork tomorrow and I have to get my things packed."

"Going back to the survey area?" Sam asked.

"I thought so," she said. "But maybe we'll try the riverside this time." She gave me an innocent look. "What do *you* think?"

"The riverside?" I managed.

"You know, by boat."

"Well . . ."

"We can rent one somewhere," she said, but Sam waved a hand.

"Alan, you've still got that john boat, don't you?"

I exhaled. "Yes, but it's for bayous. You don't want to put it in the river, for God's sake."

Sam blinked. "We did when we had that survey over at Hog Point, in, when was it? Eighty-five? You remember *that*."

"That was different. We kept close to the bank and—"

"That's what we plan to do," Pepper said, then turned to me. "Don't we?"

I felt my face go hot. "The motor's only a thirty-five. In a river like the Mississippi . . ."

"Oh, baloney," Sam snorted. "Fred Quimby and I went across the damn thing in a canoe, in '38."

"We really do have to go," I said, getting up. I turned to give Libby a hug. "Thanks for having us."

"Thank *you*," she whispered. "I can tell he's better already."

"Yes," I said. "It looks like it."

Sam took Pepper Courtney's hands in both of his.

"My dear, I hope you'll be back. But make it soon. I'm

not getting any younger." He gave a loud sigh. "You may just keep an old man alive."

The recipient of this jollity laughed and hugged him. "You'll outlive us all."

I was beginning to be afraid he would.

"Well, Alan . . ." She turned to me. But Sam put a hand on my shoulder.

"Before you go, there's something I've been meaning to show you." He drew me after him, through the parlor and the living room, to the kitchen.

"So what is it?" I asked. "Is the drain stuck?"

"No," he hissed. "That was just an excuse. I only wanted to tell you I think you've finally done it."

I stared back, blankly.

"Done what?"

"Found the right one, of course. My God, Alan, after some of the women I've seen you with. That red-haired harridan who wanted to run your life, the fat one with piano legs . . ."

"Marguerite was short, but piano legs . . ."

"And then the few nice ones, you ran off. That's why I wanted to tell you you'd better not do that this time, or I'll rise from my grave to make your life miserable."

"You're not *in* your grave," I protested. "And as far as there being anything between this Courtney woman and myself . . ."

"I know." He patted my shoulder as you would a child. "But I'm telling you Alan, she's the best one yet. Quality. Intelligence. A sense of humor. Beauty."

"Are we talking about the same person? Oh, she's bright enough, and I guess if she dressed a little bit more like a, well, a *woman*, but her personality—"

"—is delightful. She makes me feel young again. I tell you, Alan . . ."

"Just because she flattered you . . ."

He straightened his shoulders. "I didn't hear any flattery." He cleared his throat. "Well, she may be *too* good for you. I fully expect you'll toss her away just like the others." He threw up his hands.

I started out of the kitchen, but he caught my arm.

"By the way, who hired you for this survey? Anybody I know?"

I told him about T-Joe Dupont and how he'd died mysteriously.

"T-Joe Dupont?" Sam mulled over the name. "Late forties, in the oil field supply business?"

"You know him?"

"He was my student, a year or two after you. Nice boy. Loved archaeology but figured he couldn't ever make a living at it, so he went into engineering. But we kept in touch."

"Strange he didn't mention you."

"Well . . ." Sam ran a hand through his white mane. "Maybe he didn't want to embarrass you by comparing you to a superior archaeologist."

"That's probably it," I said.

"You know, he had a hell of a time with his son. The boy was into drugs, spent time in jail. Damn near broke T-Joe's heart, to have to lock up his own son."

"It must've worked," I said. "The boy's sober now."

"Is he?"

I thought of Willie's drunken performance in David's hospital room.

"Well, more or less. Anyway, he loved his father."

"Really?"

"Seems like it. Why? Is there something you aren't telling me?"

Sam sighed and shook his head.

"Just something T-Joe told me the last time I saw him."

"Which was?"

Sam cocked his head to the side and frowned.

"He said his son was furious T-Joe didn't bail him out. He said when he got out he was going to kill his father."

The drive home was silent, and when I stopped in her office parking lot she opened her door, then turned to me:

"I can't thank you enough for taking me to see Sam. He's a wonderful person." She flashed me a smile. "Good night." She started to shut the door, then held up. "What time did you want to load up the boat tomorrow?"

"I'll let you know," I said.

The door slammed and I watched her walk over to the Integra. If I hadn't known better, I'd have said she was humming. Maybe she wouldn't have been if she'd heard what Sam had said about Willie's threat against T-Joe.

▰ Sixteen

I crept in late the next morning, hoping the visit to Sam MacGregor had been part of a dream. But when I saw the white Integra in front of our office, I knew better and groaned.

"That *woman* is waiting for you," Marilyn pronounced. "If I'd known you were going to be late, I'd have sent her on her way, but she kept insisting you were going out in the boat together and—"

"It's okay," I said. "I'll handle her."

Gator looked up from the table where he was sorting artifacts and gave me a gap-toothed leer.

"You know what I mean," I said.

I walked into the room that had once been a bedroom but now served as our library.

She was seated in one of our yard-sale chairs, staring up at the shelf.

"Not bad," she said, "but there are a few big holes. You don't have a complete set of C. B. Moore . . ."

She was wearing designer jeans, a khaki shirt, and a red bandanna around her neck.

"Well, next time you're up East maybe you can find one for us at a rare book store."

She ignored the jibe and pulled a map tube up from where it had been lying on the floor.

"I thought we should decide where we're going to put in," she said. "We can either start upstream and then have to fight the current on the way back, or start downstream and fight it on the first leg.''

"There's another option," I said, picking up the map and starting toward my office. She followed and I closed the door. "We might want to rethink going at all."

"What?"

I told her then what I knew about T-Joe's murder, the tooth, and what Sam had told me about Willie's resentment against his father.

"You have a right to know," I said. "We could be walking into something."

"Well, it's nice to know finally," she said. "Though it would've been good to know before now."

"Sorry. I guess I held out, but I didn't know you'd be going back with me."

She nodded. "I'm not about to let some maniac chase me away."

I shrugged. "Then here's how I see it. There's only one trail to the water so far as I can see, without going five extra miles, and that's right here." I pointed to a dashed line on the map that came out of the woods about a half-mile above the island and ended at the water's edge. "We can try that."

And if we're lucky, I thought, there won't be anyplace to put in at all and we can stop this insanity.

"Good." She rolled the map up again and stuck it back in the tube. "I guess the boat is the metal one with a flat hull I saw behind the house?"

So she'd even scoped out our backyard.

"You didn't see another one, did you?"

I walked out of the room and called for Gator to help me load the boat.

Fifteen minutes later the boat had been lifted onto the trailer and the trailer hitched to the Blazer. Normally, I didn't like to pull loads that heavy, but most of the road was four-lane highway. I watched Dr. Pepper Courtney sling her little field bag into the back of my vehicle, then lean her head in.

"I'll go in mine," she said. "Always safer to have two vehicles, right?"

How could I complain about being deprived of her company?

By the time we'd left the interstate and slid down onto U.S. 61 I'd entertained at least three different versions of the same daydream. In one, the Integra was lying astraddle a particularly vicious pothole in the gravel track, wheels still spinning, as its driver called out for help. In the second, she was standing up in the boat, against my earnest protestations, and then falling out, into the fast-moving current. And in the third version, which I especially liked, she was ignoring my warnings and leaping blithely onto the sand surface at the foot of the bluff, only to sink hip-deep. Atop the cliff, I was calling down to ask if she'd ever visited La Brea, in Los Angeles, where all the dead animals floated up from the tar.

I was yanked from my dreaming by the sound of a horn. The Integra had slipped up beside me and she was honking, motioning for me to pull over.

The vision of a smoking wheel bearing on the trailer replaced the images of her misfortune and I eased off the accelerator.

But when I got out there was no burning smell and for a split second I thought maybe she'd been trying to point out a bulge in one of my tires. Then she opened her door and I saw she wanted me to walk up to where she'd halted, just ahead of me. We were beside the Exxon tank farm, just north of town. Not the best part of the city to stop in. The only folks who lived around here were those who the city didn't care about and many of whom, consequently, figured they didn't have a lot to lose.

"It's a phone call," she explained, holding up her car phone for me to see. "Your office."

"My office?"

"I left my cellular number with your secretary, just in case. She said you never keep yours on."

I took the receiver, wondering what could have made Marilyn call me here.

"Hello?"

Her words tumbled over themselves in the rush to get out: "I'm sorry to bother you, Alan, I really am, but she was so demanding, I didn't know what to say, and then I remembered that woman had left a number for a car phone and . . . She isn't listening, is she?"

"No. Now who called? Who are you talking about?"

"A woman." Marilyn lowered her voice to a whisper. "She came right after you left. She's in the next room. She said her name was Lesage. No, Lastrapes. Dominique Lastrapes. She was so rude I thought I better call you on the car phone."

Dominique . . . Of course: Willie's sister.

"Put her on," I sighed.

Pepper watched, interested, as I shifted the phone to my other ear.

"Client's sister," I said.

Pepper said something but the voice on the other end of the phone blotted it out.

"Dr. Graham? This is Dominique Lastrapes, Joseph Dupont's daughter. We need to talk."

"I'm here."

"You've been listening to my brother, Willie. I hear he's got you looking for this Indian treasure."

"He's asked me to do the work your father wanted done."

"Finding that treasure?"

"It's not really a treasure. I know it's called that but—"

"Dr. Graham, my brother does *not* speak for the family. He talked my mother into signing a power of attorney and used her money—our money—for this, and we know very well he doesn't have any intention of sharing the treasure with us."

I groaned to myself. "First, Mrs. Lastrapes, there isn't any treasure in the sense you're talking about, and, second, I think your brother is just trying to find out what happened to your father and why he was killed."

I heard an intake of breath over the line.

"Dr. Graham, William has pulled the wool over your eyes. But I doubt he's telling you everything."

"You mean like his time in jail?"

"Oh." A heartbeat's silence and then: "Well, I'm sure he put a good face on it, for himself. And did he tell you he was against this whole project from the start?"

"Really."

"I didn't think he did." Her triumph was unmistakable. "William thought Dad was wasting money that ought to be his when Dad died. If you can imagine that! Dad was only forty-five years old. That's looking ahead."

"Mrs. Lastrapes . . ."

"And I'm not making this up. You can ask the man who sold Dad the land, Mr. Wascom."

"Carter Wascom?"

"That's right. We were all standing there that day when Dad and Mr. Wascom made a handshake deal, even before anything was signed, and my brother threw a fit. So what do you think about that?"

"I'm an archaeologist, not a detective, Mrs. Lastrapes. But I'll look into it."

"You do that, Dr. Graham. And I should inform you that we've talked sense to my mother and the power of attorney's been rescinded. So you might as well just come back."

"We've already been paid for some of the work. I intend to finish that part," I said.

"You go ahead. But whatever you find, you remember it doesn't belong to my brother. It belongs to the whole family."

"I'll remember that. Goodbye, Mrs. Lastrapes."

I pushed the *end* button and handed Pepper the phone.

"Sounds like trouble," she said.

"Nothing like a family feud," I said. I told her what Dominique had said. "Willie may've had his ups and downs with his father, but he knows we aren't going to find anything worth a lot of money."

"So what do you want to do now?"

"His check went through, so as far as I'm concerned we're still employed."

"We?"

"Whoever. But I think it would be good to talk to Carter Wascom."

Twenty minutes later I slowed as I passed Greenbriar. It slept quietly in the morning sun, and the driveway gate was still closed. I went on to the Dupont property and pulled in, to get the boat off the road, and then got into the Integra with Pepper.

When we returned to the plantation the driveway gate was open.

We nosed into the drive and then rolled slowly toward the big house, the wheels popping the gravel as we went. She halted in front of the house.

"You sure someone's here?" she asked.

"I'm not sure of anything," I said. "But there's a car in the driveway."

We got out and started up the wooden steps toward the long front porch. A swing moved slowly in the warm air, as if propelled by a ghost, and I felt the hot breeze brush my face like fingers.

We came to the big front door and halted. It bore a black wreath, but the wreath wasn't new. We exchanged glances and I thought I saw P. E. Courtney, Ph.D., shudder.

I raised my hand, hesitated, then rapped three times.

There was silence, punctuated only by the squeaky chains of the swing. I thought of Eulalia Wascom, seated in the swing, wearing one of those Scarlett O'Hara skirts, as the people of her world reenacted a bygone era in the lamplight.

The sound of footsteps roused me from my daydreams. The door opened and a tall, light-skinned black man in a white shirt and black bow tie stared out at me from deep-set eyes.

"My name is Graham," I said. "Is Mr. Wascom in?"

"Mr. Wascom is busy right now. If you'll come in I'll ask if he can see you."

He held the door for us and showed us into a parlor. It smelled of mothballs and as we walked across the thick rug I felt dust tickling my nose. There was a snap as the light went on and I saw an old-fashioned fireplace, a stuffed sofa, and an antique coffee table. Facing the fireplace, back to us, was a tall easy chair, as if placed there for the warmth of the blaze. The windows, however, were shuttered and the atmosphere of the room stuffy, so that sweat was already beading my forehead and arms.

The servant pointed to the sofa. "Please sit down."

We looked at each other and shook our heads at the same time.

"I think we'll stand," I said.

Another little bow of acknowledgment and the old man vanished back into the hallway. I turned to P. E., but she was looking at something else, and I followed her eyes.

The oil portrait over the fireplace was of a woman. And there was no doubt, from the antebellum attire, and the dark, piercing eyes, that we were looking at a painting of Eulalia Wascom.

"My God," P. E. breathed, "she's beautiful."

I regarded the slightly rounded face, the almost catlike eyes, and the long, onyx hair, and I nodded.

"Yes," I agreed. "She was."

"She's dead?"

"For four years now," I said. "She was Carter Wascom's wife."

"She was more than that," a voice said from behind me. "She was my life."

We turned together and saw Carter Wascom in the doorway, motionless. He wore tight-fitting blue jeans and a blue workshirt, open at the neck, and there was a smudge of dirt on his forehead.

"Mr. Wascom," I said, and took a step toward him. "I'm Alan Graham. We met the other day. This is Dr. Courtney. She's an archaeologist, too."

"Pleasure." He gave me a cold hand and then released my own after the first shake, as if the warmth of living flesh had burned him and gave Pepper a stiff little bow. "I'm sorry I kept you waiting, but this isn't a very good day, I'm afraid."

"I'm sorry."

He turned to the manservant, standing behind him.

"I think it's deep enough now, Louis. I'll be there in a

minute and we can finish." He turned back to us: "I was digging a grave."

"A grave?" I asked.

"Balfour, the black Lab you saw with us the other day. He belonged to Eulalia. The last living link to her, really, besides myself. I loved that dog." He gave a little shake of his head.

"I'm sorry," I said.

"Thank you."

"How did the dog die?" Pepper asked.

For a split second Wascom looked startled.

"I think it was a snake bite," he said. "I found him behind the house this morning." He sighed.

"We won't bother you for very long, then," I said. "I just needed to ask you a question about the deal you made with T-Joe Dupont."

"Oh?"

"I understand he and his family came up here together to look at the land and afterward you and he made a handshake agreement?"

Wascom frowned. "That's correct."

"And his son, Willie, was there at the time?"

"Oh, yes." Wascom nodded. "I thought he and his father were going to come to blows."

"Really."

"Willie thought his father was paying too much. I don't think he liked the idea from the start. He said the oil market wasn't good enough, this wasn't the old days, that his father was still acting like it was 1975." Wascom gave his brittle little laugh. "As if he remembered 1975."

"I see. Well, thank you for your time. We're sorry about the dog."

"Life is so fragile," Wascom said, cocking his head slightly. "Don't you think?"

"It is," I said, waiting.

"People can be robust one minute, in the flower of health, and the next . . ." He shook his head. "I used to believe in God, Mr. Graham. I don't anymore. No deity could be so cruel . . ." I noticed that his eyes were on the portrait now. "Isn't she beautiful? I had that painted the first year we were married. I paid quite a lot for it. It captures her spirit. She was such a vivacious lady."

I was feeling chills despite the closeness of the room.

"Mr. Wascom . . ."

"I wish you'd tell me what you're doing for the Duponts," he said. "I hear you're looking for something."

I nodded. "T-Joe wanted an archaeological survey and Willie asked us to follow through. He's interested in Indian culture. That's the work we do."

Wascom frowned. "Indian culture. You mean you're looking for artifacts?"

"That's right."

"I see." He walked across the room, head down, and then raised it suddenly to fix me with his dead eyes.

"You know, that was my family's land."

"Yes, sir."

"Eulalia never would have let me sell it to someone outside the family. Not one square inch."

"What about Marcus Briney?"

Wascom blinked. "Oh, well, Marcus is sort of a guardian. Used to be up at Angola, you know. Keeps an eye on the place."

"He claims he wasn't at home when T-Joe Dupont was killed."

"No, that's right. He passed us in his truck, coming from town, after I found the wreck."

"This road makes a horseshoe, though, doesn't it? A person could go out to the highway taking the northern route, and then come back this way."

"But he didn't. I saw him leave earlier that morning. Why?"

"Just trying to make sense of things," I said. "Thank you, Mr. Wascom."

"By the way," P. E. asked. "Have you seen Absalom Moon?"

Wascom's thin brows went up a half-inch. "Absalom? Not for a week or so. But that isn't strange. He comes and goes. Why?" He took a step toward us. "Is something wrong?"

"No," she said quickly. "We were just looking for him."

"Well, if there's nothing else?" he asked.

"No. Thanks for your time," I said, and we started for the door. I pulled it open and gulped in the fresh air from the hallway.

"Come back," Wascom called from behind us. "Come back and see us, you hear?" He started toward us, then stopped.

"I'll have Louis make some iced tea. I . . ." He gazed around him in confusion.

The manservant appeared from nowhere and took Wascom's shoulder.

"I've put Balfour in, Mr. Carter. I wrapped him up in Miss Eulalia's blanket like you wanted. You can come say some words now, if you'd like."

Wascom nodded.

"Balfour. Yes, of course."

We slipped out. It was good to get out of the suffocating old house and into the sun.

SEVENTEEN

It was five minutes before either of us spoke and then P. E. said, "Strange."

"I don't like it, either," I said, as she halted her car in the field, by the boat trailer. "Wascom isn't telling us everything."

"I had the same feeling. But what do you think he's holding out?"

"I don't know. But what's so worth protecting that he needs Marcus Briney living next door?"

"You think Briney could be the killer, then?"

"I don't know what the motive would be. Besides, Carter just told us Briney wasn't there, at least when T-Joe was killed."

"A point," she said.

I opened my door.

"You may want to leave your car here," I said. "The roads can be pretty rugged in these parts."

"Good idea." She locked up, then came around to the Blazer and got in on the passenger side.

"Want to stop and see if Absalom ever came home?" she asked.

"Sure."

But he hadn't. The place was as deserted as ever and I had a bad feeling about it. Worse, the sky had clouded and I knew an afternoon thunderstorm might make a muddy slop of the road. All I could think to do was to find the track, and if it looked like a trap, to come back out and go boating some other day.

P. E. pulled out a topographic map. "According to the map the trail to the river is about a mile from here," she said.

As we curved up the road, heading north now with the river somewhere to our left beyond the trees, I caught a glimpse the stacks of the nuclear plant. Could there be any truth to Carter Wascom's accusations? The plant had been plagued by shutdowns and safety problems. But only a complete medical study could say whether any waste product could have harmed his wife. I was just an archaeologist, not a physician or a nuclear engineer.

We passed the end of the fence and were alone now in a long tunnel of trees. All at once I began to doubt my sanity. What was I doing here, getting ready to take a small boat down to the Father of Waters? It was as harebrained a notion as any I'd ever succumbed to. We could be capsized, carried away by the current, we could—

"Here it is," she said and I saw a narrow dirt road heading off to the left. I braked to a halt.

"Do we really want to do this?" I asked.

"I think you can make it," she said.

My hands tightened on the wheel.

"Let's hope," I said and turned left, onto the dirt.

It took twenty minutes to bump our way down from the hills to the floodplain. The ruts were dry, and I knew they'd fill up quickly in a good rain. The sky was still blurred by clouds. How the hell was I going to explain it if we got stuck?

"Why are you going so slowly?" she asked. "Is the hitch loose?"

I recalled the split-moment of vulnerability I'd seen a few days ago in her office. To think that I'd almost been lulled into sympathy!

I wrenched the wheel to avoid a hole in the road and waited for her comment but, surprisingly, there wasn't any. She was looking out the window now, an odd, almost fixated stare.

"Something the matter?" I asked.

She gave a little shake of her head.

"I don't know. It was *déjà vu*. I had the sudden feeling I'd been here before." She turned her head around to face me. "I think that portrait of Eulalia Wascom spooked me. Does that sound crazy?"

"No, it's a spooky place," I said. "Him living like that, in a dream world, with nothing but a big picture." I made a low, wailing sound. "Maybe she's in the car with us now."

"You're making fun of me."

"Never."

We came down onto the floodplain then and I saw a wet patch ahead. I gunned the engine and we bumped through it. As we neared the river, the temperature rose, along with my sense of uneasiness.

"Can't you run up the windows and put on the air?" she asked.

"We can run up the windows," I said, "but the only air you're going to get is from outside. The unit's broken."

"Oh, God," she muttered.

I sloughed through another puddle. "We could've brought your Integra," I said.

"That's very funny."

We came up a slight rise that I recognized as the natural levee of the river and then it was in front of us, a mile wide of choppy, gray water, all snags and whirlpools and logs headed for the Gulf.

I stopped and got out, a warm breeze hitting me in the face. The banks here were covered with rip-rap, broken rocks dumped by the Corps of Engineers to retard erosion. On either side of us were trees, mostly oaks, with a few willows at water's edge. I calculated for a few minutes how I'd turn the rig around, then got back in.

"What now?" she asked.

"I'm going to try to back this rig down to the water," I said, not bothering to complain about the rip-rap and how hard it would be to stand on it without twisting an ankle. I managed to turn in the little clearing and then backed toward the river. When I was as far as I dared go, I cut the engine and put on the hand brake.

I got out and motioned for her to stand on the other side of the trailer, then unfastened the cables holding the boat in place, and together we pulled the boat backward until it was half out of the trailer and half hanging in air. I made sure the outboard motor was cocked up so that the propeller wouldn't strike the rip-rap and then together we eased the boat down onto the rocks. I reached into the boat and tossed her an orange life vest.

"Put that on," I said, picking up one for myself. I went back, got my field pack from the Blazer, and put it into the boat. Then I locked the Blazer and went back to the boat, threading my GPS unit onto my belt.

"A *Trailblazer*?" she asked.

"I know," I told her: "You have one with a map display that can give you accuracy within ten meters."

"Two meters," she said smugly.

I patted my global positioning unit. "Well, I've done okay with this one," I said, thinking of the days when we'd had to reckon from maps instead of satellites.

We manhandled the aluminum hull down the uneven slope, and over the rocks until the stern touched the water and began to float. Without being told, she got in as I held the gunwale steady. I checked. The paddles were inside, and so were the oil and gas cans. I shoved the bow until the entire boat was floating and then pulled it until it was parallel to the bank.

"Come up front," I said and waited while she scrambled toward the bow. Then I stepped into the stern, by the motor, and began to pour in the oil and gas mixture that the outboard required. There wasn't any current here, a few feet from the bank, because the water was shallow, but twenty feet away, where the bank dropped off, I saw sticks and debris racing past.

I was crazy to be doing this. Totally, irremediably, hopelessly crazy.

"Hold on," I said, and pulled the cord to start the motor.

The big Johnson roared to life and the boat surged forward. I steered away from the bluffs and into the current.

It caught us and in seconds we were skimming past the shore. I kept the throttle low, staying as close to the banks as I could without brushing the drift that had piled up against the land. Ahead, a mile away, was the island, just a smudge of tree line against the darker background of the hills. I looked up at the sky. The clouds were darker now and I didn't like the smell in the air. A normal summer storm ought to boil up in the early afternoon and be done in half an hour, but it was late morning and the clouds were already there.

She must have seen them, too, because she looked up and called something back to me, but her words were taken by the wind.

Water slapped the aluminum sides and once the prow slammed into a submerged limb, sending shudders vibrating back along the hull. I was thinking about the convicts now, braving these currents. *The river was forty-five feet deep at Baton Rouge, and they hadn't found their bodies yet...*

The island was just ahead of us now and I thought for a second of the little brass bell pressing into my thigh from its place in my pocket. I was beginning to feel sorry I'd ever found it.

She was pointing and I nodded: The place where we'd stood when the chase team had descended on us was ahead of us now, and I guided us toward the white beach. The nose of the boat gave a bump and P. E. jumped out onto the sand and grabbed the painter line, holding us steady as I cut the engine. The boat sloughed around like a big clock hand going backward until it came to rest against the shore, stern downstream, and I jumped onto the land and ran to help her pull the line and nudge the hull up onto the beach so that the boat was secured from the current.

"You've been in boats before," I said.

She brushed blond hair out of her face. "I did a marine survey of the Ohio River in my second year," she said. "And I've had some experience since then."

I should have known.

"Where are you going?" she called, as I started up the eroded sand slope.

I didn't answer, just scrambled to the top and waited as she followed. I stuck out a hand and she hesitated, then took it and let me pull her up. It wasn't far from where I'd found the little bell.

"Well, how do you want to search?" she asked. I noticed a single drop of perspiration on her forehead and watched it roll down until she reached up and wiped it away.

"Each take an area?" I suggested, setting my GPS unit on the ground to take a reading of our position for future reference.

"Fine. I'll take this area right here," she said.

I blinked. "I was thinking *I'd* take this one."

"That's all right. I think you'd be happier over in the woods," she said. "And I'm just a woman, so right here's fine, where it's clear, along the bank."

"I thought you'd want to have the woods, so you could prove you're up to it," I said.

She folded her arms. "Of course, there's another option."

"Oh?"

"You could show me what you picked up the other day," she said. "You know, what you called a cartridge case."

My mouth must have come open because there was a smug look on her face.

"I—" But she cut me off:

"You probably have it on you now, don't you? Was it really a brass casing or was it something else?"

Eagle eye.

"I never said it was a brass casing," I protested. "You did."

"Well, whatever it was, you seemed in a hurry to get it into your pocket, so you must have thought it was important."

I managed an exaggerated shrug. "It wasn't *in situ*, I mean, it could have gotten here all kinds of ways. The water, somebody dropping it, somebody reburying it in the sand . . ."

"Can I see this *it*?"

With a sigh I reached into my pants pocket and brought out the little paper-wrapped object. "No big deal," I said, handing it to her.

She unwrapped it and her eyes went wide. "No. Of course not. Just an eighteenth-century trade bell. The kind the French gave to the Tunica. Just the kind that popped up in a hundred burials twenty miles north of here. No, nothing much. Might as well throw it in the river."

"Sarcasm is unnecessary."

"Oh, was I being sarcastic?" She handed back the artifact. "Excuse me. Maybe I don't like having data held out on me. Maybe it's just that I don't like being treated like a first-year graduate student, by the all-wise professor, the . . ."

I ignored her and went over to the place in the bank where I'd found the bell. I squatted and examined the surface. There was no evidence of recent rooting by animals or people, but it was sand, which meant after a few days any marks would be gone. The ground was littered with brass shell casings, mostly .22s, but a few .30-30s and two or three plastic shotgun shells. I went down to the boat and got my trowel out of my pack and began to probe the ground with the sharp point.

A shadow fell over my shoulder and I looked up.

"Try the metal detector," she said, pointing to the boat.

I shook my head. "It'll pick up every shell casing for three feet around."

She said nothing, just went down to the boat for her own pack and came back with a trowel of her own. She got down on hands and knees a few yards away and, wordlessly, began to probe the ground methodically, working in a square about three feet on a side.

I stood up. "We'd better divide this up," I said resignedly, and began to draw lines in the sand, marking off rough squares. "You take the ones south of there . . ." I indicated one of the lines I'd drawn. "I'll take the others."

And don't, I started to add, *cross over my line.*

By noon our search had turned up nothing and all I had for my own trouble was sore knees. The sky showed no sign of clearing and I sensed that the temperature had dropped a few degrees.

"We can go back to my vehicle and eat," I suggested.

"You didn't bring your lunch?" she responded. "I thought that was what was in the cooler."

"It is. I was thinking about if there was rain," I said.

"I can stand rain," she said. "I have—"

"I know," I broke in. "A fold-up poncho in your pack and an inflatable house."

"No house, but you were right about the poncho."

I went to the cooler, got out my sandwich and a Dr. Pepper, and watched her dig in her pack. She came out with a can of sardines and some crackers. Probably very healthy, I reflected, as I searched for some shade so I could eat my ham and cheese. She came over and sat down on the ground across from me.

"Kind of reminds me of Huckleberry Finn," she said.

I looked up. "The river, you mean."

"The river, me, you, looking for something buried. It's the kind of thing Huck and Tom and Jim would do."

"Right. Well, it's the same river and I guess people are pretty much the same."

"If it wasn't Briney who killed T-Joe, it *had* to be either Willie Dupont or Wascom," she said suddenly. "They both have guns. You said Willie had one when he took you and David onto the property the first time."

I shrugged. "I'm not sure about Willie. The pistol he had wasn't a .22, but that doesn't mean much. Almost everybody down here has an arsenal with a .22 in it somewhere. Besides, why pay us money to do a survey?"

"So we can find whatever's really buried here and he can get his hands on it, maybe."

"I thought about that. But I keep thinking about what he told me in the office when he came to meet us: He said he figured if we did the survey, we'd find out who killed his father. Doesn't sound like a murderer to me."

"Wascom then?"

I nodded. "Wascom's definitely a quart low. Whether he'd shoot anybody with that rifle of his, I don't know." I finished my sandwich and bit into my apple.

"Do you think he's the one who chased us in the woods?"

"Hard to say. But offhand he doesn't look the type. I can't see Carter Wascom getting all hot and sweaty back in the hills, for one thing."

"Not if he knew what he was doing. But what if it was in some kind of, well, trance?"

"All things are possible." I got up and dusted off my clothes. "Maybe we ought to search the beach ridges," I suggested.

She digested the notion and then hopped up. "Good idea."

We went to the sloping bank, where the sands stretched down to the water's edge in deep, eroded valleys where water had run from the top of the bluff down into the river. It was always possible something had fallen out of the sand, into one of the three-foot-deep ravines.

It was tough work, because we had to stand straddling each valley and examine the ground under us visually. The only progress was to hop from one sand valley to the next, and after nearly an hour my legs were losing their spring.

At just after two the first raindrops spattered against the sand. I glanced at the low, heavy clouds. There was no thunder and maybe the rain would pass over, but I wouldn't bet on it. We'd moved down the beach about a quarter of a mile south of the boat, to a place where the willows had died away, leaving an open spot, and I began to think it was time to get back. The pace of the raindrops quickened and I looked over at my companion.

But P. E. Courtney appeared oblivious to the weather.

I knew then that she was a fanatic.

She finally produced a flimsy plastic poncho and I went back to the boat and dug my own poncho out of my pack. I hoped the rain would pass quickly, because visibility was down and the river was no place to be when you were running blind.

I walked back to where she was down on hands and knees, peering into one of the crevasses.

"I think it was a fluke," I said.

She peered up at me through rain-streaked glasses.

"A fluke?"

"The little bell. I think it washed up here from somewhere else, because there isn't anything else where it was found and this island is new."

She pondered for a few seconds. "Then that means it came from someplace upstream."

"Someplace," I said.

"Maybe we should look for that place."

"Where?" I asked. "There's a thousand miles of river."

"Realistically, though, there's only a few miles," she said. "For that kind of artifact, for the time period, it must have been between where the Red River enters the Mississippi and here. That's only thirty river miles."

"Only?" I shook my head. "Besides, there's another possibility."

"Oh?"

"Somebody dropped it."

"Who? Absalom?"

"He'd be a good bet."

"Then where did *he* get it?" She stood up slowly. "I mean, you don't walk around with things like that. Maybe he found it inland, closer to the bluffs, where we were."

It had occurred to me. If true, it meant the main burial spot was on the highlands, closer to Greenbriar itself.

"Let's look a little more," she said. "I want to be very sure about this. Sometimes geomorphologists make mistakes. And not all maps are accurate."

I gave a little head shake. We were here now, so what the hell?

As I walked transects, with her on my right and the river fifty yards to *her* right, I thought about the time at Fort Polk, in western Louisiana, when I'd had to cut my way through a solid briar thicket in the middle of July. When I'd come out of the thicket, there'd been a clearcut in front of me three hundred yards across, full of fallen trees, burned stumps, and mud. I often told people that job was the most miserable I'd ever experienced. But now, in the sauna of the poncho, with wet fronds brushing my face, water seeping down into my boots, and a crazy woman goading me on, I thought maybe this would be my pet war story for the future.

All it would take now to complete the experience would be to step on a snake.

I checked my watch again. It was three-thirty.

I halted in my tracks.

"Enough."

She crashed through a stand of ferns fifty feet away, a woman with a mission.

"*Enough,*" I said again, this time in a loud voice.

She emerged from the ferns and turned a hooded head in my direction.

"Say something?" she called above the dripping of the forest.

"I said it's time to get the hell out of here," I yelled back. "It'll be too dark to see in the woods in a couple of hours. With the rain it's already dark. Back to the boat."

"One more transect?" she suggested.

"No. It's going to be a bitch enough getting upstream. We go now."

I saw her shoulders sag slightly. "All right."

I slopped my way through the trees toward the gray sheet that was the river. The rain was steady now, a light spatter of drops that pocked the water and hung a cloud over the far bank.

The tip of the island, where the boat was, a quarter-mile away, blurred into a gray haze. I couldn't see the boat at all.

The waves lapped at the beach, ten feet below, and a log with a red rope around it nudged the shore.

A red rope. I blinked.

"Look." She was pointing, because she saw it, too.

We scrambled down the sandy slope together and stood looking down at the object before us.

It wasn't a log at all, but the body of a man. The rope wasn't a rope, but red suspenders. And I knew where I'd seen those red suspenders last: They'd been worn by the man we were searching for, Absalom Moon.

EIGHTEEN

"He must have fallen in or been dumped someplace upstream," I said.

She stared up at me. "What do you think we should do?"

"Drag him up on the bank and then call the sheriff."

She nodded. "Right."

I reached down, found his belt loops, and tugged while she pulled at his shoulders. Between us, we got him half onto the beach and then managed with our next effort to pull him the rest of the way. The body was waterlogged, paler than it had been in life, and when I turned him over I saw the river creatures had done a job on his face. Or maybe he'd been hit by a ship's propeller. It didn't much matter at this point.

She stooped and washed her hands in the river and I knelt beside her.

"It's murder, isn't it?" she said.

I shrugged. "Probably. But he could've fallen in. It'll take an autopsy. Let's see your phone."

She pulled it out of her pocket and punched the *on* button.

Nothing happened.

She gave me a guilty look.

"I forgot to charge it last night."

"Then I reckon we'd better get back to the boat."

We made our way to the top of the bank and then started toward the point of the island. I knew the temperature

142

hadn't changed but it suddenly felt colder and a chill passed over me.

When we reached the point the chill became a deep freeze.

The boat was gone.

"Could it have slid back down into the river and floated away?" she asked.

I shook my head. "Not likely. I think somebody pushed it."

We stared at each other.

"Then whoever killed Absalom is nearby."

"Maybe," I said and bent to look at the ground. The sand was a confusion of boot tracks and drag marks from the boat and it was hard for me to tell if there were any tracks besides our own.

I thought of the frequent river traffic: tugboats with barges, launches, dredge boats. They could all generate waves that could lift a small boat. But nothing had passed since we'd been out here, unless it had been on the far side of the river, during the rain. A wave traveling from that distance would have weakened too much to do anything, though.

I stood up and looked at the misty hills. It would be a long trek, in near darkness. My pack had been left in the boat, with my compass, GPS, and flip phone.

"What now?" she asked and for only the second time since I'd known her I thought I noticed hesitancy.

"I don't know," I admitted. She started down the slope toward me and all of a sudden the sand slid out from under her and she gave a little cry of pain. When I got to her she was sitting on the beach, holding her ankle.

"Damn, damn, damn," she swore softly. "I think I sprained it."

I bent down beside her. "Did you feel something pop?"

"No, but it hurts like hell. Let me sit here for a minute."

I nodded. "I've twisted my ankle before," I said. "I know how it feels."

"That doesn't help." She reached out to me: "Here, give me a hand up."

I bent and put my hand under her arm, and she struggled to her feet. For a few seconds she hesitated and then she slowly transferred her weight back to the injured ankle.

She gave a little yelp and raised her hurt leg.

"It's no good," she said. "Lower me back down."

I let her settle slowly onto the sand. She sat there for a moment, rubbing her ankle and then she uttered a little cry of despair.

"Well, I've made a real mess of it," she lamented. "Now we're stuck."

"It can't be helped," I said.

"Aren't you mad at me?"

"Did you do it on purpose?"

"Of course not. But I acted like such a b—"

"Yes?"

"Anyway, I'm sorry."

I nodded, then reached down and grabbed her arm again. "Come on, I'll help you to the top of the bank."

She gave me her arm and grabbed me around the waist. Together we struggled up the west bank, my knees sinking into the sand, until we were both crawling our way upward. When we got there we sat side by side, panting.

"You'll have to leave me here," she said.

"No way we'll stay until morning. Together."

"Are you sure?"

"Yes." I spotted her pack a few feet away, on the ground. "Do you by any chance have any matches in there?"

"Sure. And a penlight."

"Good. I'll get some wood. Do you have a knife or anything we can scrape off the wet bark with?"

"A hunting knife," she said. "Are you going to try to make a fire?"

"No, I'm going to *make* a fire." I checked my watch. Four o'clock and the rain was still falling.

I went to the trees and began to hunt for dry wood. I wished I felt as confident about being able to make a fire as I'd sounded. Here and there, though, where sticks and branches lay facedown on the ground, I was able to feel a dry side and I dragged the bits and pieces out to where she sat and took off my poncho and covered them.

"You're going to get soaked," she warned.

"I'm already soaked," I said. "Besides, we need a fire. It'll keep away the insects, and any boat that's passing will see it. Then we can use the flashlight to signal."

"And the person that took the boat?"

"I'm hoping they escaped in it," I said.

She looked up at me and nodded doubtfully, then pointed to her pack.

"There's something else in there," she said. "An army survival manual."

"Where did you get that?"

"It was my brother's. He was in Desert Storm. I kind of held on to it."

I went to her pack and felt around until I found it, a small, brown paperback book in a plastic pouch. I glanced over the contents. How to tell directions without a compass, how to live off the land, how to make a fire . . . I slipped it back into the pouch and put the pouch back into the pack.

"I'll use it if I have trouble," I said. "Right now, about all we can do is hope the rain stops."

I sat down next to her on the sand. A few seconds later she struggled out of her poncho and handed me an edge. "Put it over your head," she said. "We can both fit."

I felt her warmth against me and listened to the steady patter of raindrops on the plastic. "I guess we should have left earlier, when you wanted," she said. "I'm sorry."

"No use crying about it now," I told her.

"I just get so wrapped up in my work . . . I love archaeology. I really do."

"So do I. It's a character flaw."

"But you're a man. It's harder for a woman. I had to fight every step of the way. How can you get men to take you seriously when you've got a name like Pepper? They all think it's so cute. *Pepper Ellen.* What a nice little girl."

"You're talking about people like Oldham. Well, we aren't all that way. And sometimes, when we get the feeling somebody's pressing too hard, well . . ."

"Yeah." She rubbed her ankle. "I feel like it's swelling." She started to unlace her boot.

I helped her loosen the boot and touched her ankle. She flinched.

"Can you move it?"

"I don't know," she said, but I saw her foot move slightly up and down and then from side to side.

"I don't think it's broken," I said. "The best thing to do is wait for the swelling to go down and then try to put some weight on it."

"Yes, Doctor," she said with a grimace. "So what do we do if a boat doesn't pick us up?"

"I don't know." But I thought of our flight through the hills, with our unseen pursuer throwing things at us from above. I didn't look forward to a repeat of the episode, trying to support *her* with one arm. "I'll think of something," I said. "Maybe Marx has a quotation for the occasion."

"Marx?" She turned her head to look at me. "Oh, I see: You think from what I said last night about the slaves building the levees that I'm a Marxist."

"It was in fashion when I was a graduate student," I said.

"It still is in some places. And I think he was right about some things. But I don't go much for *isms* of any kind. Besides, I was trying to get to you."

Her admission caught me by surprise. "Why?"

"You seemed so together, so sure of everything. Like you thought you were my uncle, giving advice to this little girl."

"Your uncle?" I snorted. "I've been called a lot of things . . ."

"I'm sorry. I didn't mean to insult you."

A small river of water coursed down a crevasse in the plastic covering and started to drip on my leg.

"No insult." I sighed. "I'm just feeling my age."

"You're not old," she protested. "Not more than ten years older than I am. Well, fifteen at most."

I sucked in my stomach without thinking. "More or less."

The pattern of raindrops on the river had become barely discernible. I held out my hand. The rain had subsided into a fine mist.

I crawled out from under the cover and began to work on the pile of wood, trimming off the wet bark with the knife and trying to shave the dry places into tinder.

"Want a suggestion?" she asked.

"No."

"Try my field book," she said, reaching into her pack. "It has a lot of blank pages."

"Why didn't I think of that?"

It was a new surveyor's transit book, the kind that costs fifteen bucks, with waterproof pages, but except for the first few leaves, the rest was blank and I ripped them out and crumpled them. I arranged my dry wood over them, small pieces first, and then got out one of her matches and lit the paper. The paper flared and I watched the bright flame eat away at the paper, then die into ashes. I cursed under my breath and lit another match. By the fifth match I was beginning to think it was useless, but then some of the smaller twigs caught and then the tinder, and in a few more minutes I had a small fire.

"I'll go get some more pieces of wood," I said, taking her penlight. "It ought to be able to dry out if I put it closer to the fire."

She scuttled over to the side of the blaze and I sat down beside her.

It wouldn't be so bad, I told myself, if only we had some food. And if we could forget about the dead man a few hundred yards down the beach.

"I feel like Robinson Crusoe," she said. "Do you really think a boat will pass?"

"I don't know. All we can do is listen."

She shuddered. "This isn't like the Charles River. This is so big it scares you. It's almost like there might be things in the depths, things that are waiting to come up . . ."

I didn't say anything because I'd often had the same thought.

Finally I turned to look at her outline, faintly limned by the firelight.

"Pepper, why did you really come down here?" I asked.

"I . . ." She started to answer then stopped and picked up a small twig and broke it.

"It won't do any good to tell me it was because of some economic analysis you did. You knew what a hard time you'd have before you ever got down here, am I right?"

She nodded silently, like a child caught out in a lie.

"So what was it? You running from a bad love affair? It's understandable, you know. Nothing to be ashamed of."

"It wasn't that," she said in a voice almost too low to hear. "I'm not running away, I'm looking."

"Looking?"

She nodded. Something plopped into the water and I saw her flinch.

"I was born in 1964," she said. "Just before the Vietnam War got going good."

She drew a haphazard line in the sand with the twig.

"He went to the war," I said softly.

"Yes. In 1969, when I was five years old. He never came back."

"I'm sorry."

"Thanks. It left me and my mom and my brother, Chad. Chad was two years older than I was. We were close. He always looked after me. He was affected by dad's death worse than I was. He always said he wanted to join the army, be like him."

I waited, listening.

"His chance came in 1985, when he finished college. He went off to the service and took airborne training. He came home on leave and he seemed to like what he was doing, almost like he was proving something. Then Iraq invaded Kuwait and we sent troops over to Desert Storm. He came back with a chestful of medals but he was never the same."

"Was he wounded?"

"Not physically. But he had a wild look, a restlessness. Inside of a year he'd quit the army and was driving trucks. First we heard from him every few weeks and then we stopped hearing from him at all. When Mom died I tried to get the news to him but nobody had heard of him at his last address."

A breeze picked up and I heard the leaves of the trees rustle.

"Did you try the company he worked for?" I asked, but I thought I had a pretty good idea.

"The last record they had showed he'd delivered his cargo to New Orleans and then got another driver to take his rig back. As for him, well, he just disappeared."

"Were the police called?"

"They couldn't do anything. People disappear all the time. They said it wasn't criminal. He was an adult."

"So he just dropped off the face of the earth."

She nodded. "That is, until my third year in graduate school. That year, I got a postcard. It didn't have a word written on it, just my name and address. It went to my apartment in Cambridge and I found it in the mailbox one weekend. It was mailed from Monroe, Louisiana, and the address was in his handwriting."

I exhaled. "Are you sure?"

"Absolutely. Besides, what other possibility is there? Who'd go to so much trouble for a joke? No, I'm sure it was from him. It was his way of letting me know he was still alive but for some reason he couldn't make himself write any message."

"So when you finished school, you decided to try to hunt him up."

"Yes."

"How did your father die?" I asked.

She swallowed hard. "I'm not sure. He never came back from Nam."

"And you're thinking it had an effect on your brother."

She nodded.

And maybe, I thought, *you're thinking whatever it is that made him crack, you may have it, too.*

"Is it stupid to feel this way?" she asked.

I shook my head. "It's not stupid at all."

I held out my hand. The misting had stopped and I pulled off the poncho and laid it on the wet sand. We moved onto it and I reached over and put another limb on the fire.

"Now I understand why you're in archaeology," I said.

She gave me a funny look. "What do you mean?"

"Looking for your brother. It fits, doesn't it? Hunting for things and hunting for people?"

"I never thought of that. Anyway, archaeology's a science. It's . . ."

"Yes?" I gave her my wise-owl look.

"Oh, never mind. Maybe you're right."

She really wasn't as hard to take as I'd thought. Maybe all she needed was the guidance of a wiser colleague.

"Not that it isn't scientific," I lectured. "But there's a difference between being scientific and being a science. The New Archaeology . . ."

"The New Archaeology is thirty years old," she said dryly. "Just like hippies and antiwar demonstrations."

"I was only going to say it wasn't all that new," I huffed.

"Well, I think I attended that lecture," she said demurely.

I shot her a venomous look and saw she was smiling.

"You're impossible," I said.

"Not impossible, just a challenge," she said obliquely. "Now that you've heard about me, what about yourself? Why did you end up in contract archaeology? Didn't you ever want to teach?"

"I did once. University of New Mexico. But it didn't work out."

"Trouble with your colleagues?"

"No. With a woman."

"Mind if I ask who she was?"

I shrugged. "An archaeologist. We met in Mexico on a project. I married her. But it didn't work."

She was staring at me now. "So that explains it."

"What?"

"I thought you just had a thing against women professionals. It's really because she was an archaeologist . . ."

The words rocked me and I couldn't think of anything to say. My God, was she right? Had I struck sparks with her because of Felicia?

"I'm sorry," she said. "I talk too much sometimes."

"It's okay," I said.

She looked off into the darkness and I followed her eyes to where the flames cast dancing shadows on the looming trees.

"Do you think this could really be an old Tunica cemetery?" she asked. "I can't get rid of the feeling that they're around us. It's ridiculous, I know. I mean, it's almost as bad as being superstitious, and I can trace the reasons for it. It's just—"

"It's just that you're like every other archaeologist in the world," I said. "You have an imagination."

I stared into the trees, whose branches seemed to be beckoning as the shadows played their tricks.

"For whatever it's worth," I told her, "I feel it, too."

For a frozen instant I thought I could make out the forms of warriors, watching, bows in their hands, trying to make up their minds whether these new beings with white skins were gods or demons, trying to decide whether the people by the fire were the future, and whether that future meant power to the tribe or its annihilation. For the briefest moment I was Tonti the Iron Hand, in search of LaSalle, and the shadows were people who had been dead nearly four hundred years.

"Alan," Pepper said, breaking into my reverie.

"Yes?"

One of the shadow-warriors moved and I felt Pepper stiffen beside me.

I watched as he stepped out of my imagination and walked slowly to the other side of the fire.

Only it wasn't a bow he was carrying but a rifle. And I'd seen him before, this warrior, only yesterday.

He'd been arranging artifacts in a display case in the museum on the Tunica Reservation. His name was Ben Picote.

"Just stay where you are," he said.

NINETEEN

Pepper's hand clamped my arm.

"What's the gun for?" I managed.

"I ask the questions," Ben answered. "What are you doing here?"

"Waiting till morning," I said. "Somebody stole our boat."

For a moment the only sound was the crackle of the fire.

"I took your boat," he said finally.

"Did you kill the old man?" I tried to keep my voice calm.

"I didn't kill nobody. I saw him on the beach, though. How do I know *you* didn't kill him?"

"He's been dead awhile," I said. "We just got here."

"But you've been here before."

I nodded. "We were here when you chased us through the creek bed."

He tried to keep his face impassive but I could tell from the flicker along his jaw that my guess had scored.

"Why?" I asked, but I thought I already knew.

"You're archaeologists," he said. "You came here to dig up our dead."

I shook my head. "We came to find where the burial ground was, if there is one, but we told the land owner we wouldn't dig them up. It's against the law."

He spat on the ground, a tall, skinny kid trying to show his manhood. "When did that ever stop you people? Do you think we don't know about the bones they keep hidden in that museum down in Baton Rouge? About the burials they dug up at Bloodhound Hill, at Angola? About what you did at Trudeau? Do you think I didn't know what you were all about in the museum when you tried to bullshit LeMoine?''

Pepper gave me a shocked look.

"You know each other?"

I nodded. "This is Ben Picote. He works for Frank LeMoine, the curator at the Tunica-Biloxi museum.''

"Oh," Pepper said, letting her hand fall from my arm. "Well, I understand your feeling. I mean . . .''

"You understand?" His lip curled into a sneer. "How can you understand anything?''

"I know what it is to feel incomplete because I lost something. My father left when I was very young . . .''

"I'm talking about a million fathers. You people ran us out of this place, and now you want to come back and pull our dead out of the ground.''

"Well," I said, "we haven't found any evidence that there *are* any dead here, except for old Absalom. Any idea who killed him?''

"No, but I don't care. He was stealing from our graves. Whatever happened, he deserved.''

"You'd better care, Ben," I told him. "You just described a pretty good motive for killing him.''

Ben frowned as if this had only just occurred to him.

"How did you get here, anyway?" I asked, struggling for some kind of rapport. "Marksville's a good little distance.''

"I came by boat," he said, and I detected a trace of pride in his voice. "I drove down to the Old River Control Structure and put in there. I got a fifty-horse on my skiff. I've crossed over here lots of times. I've been to Trudeau. I've even been inside the grounds of the prison, to Bloodhound Hill, and they never even knew it.''

"That's pretty impressive," I allowed.

"So what are you going to do now?" Pepper asked.

His answer was a thrust with his gun. "Stand up," he ordered.

I helped Pepper to her feet and waited. He came around the fire, staying an arm's length away.

"Turn your pockets inside out," he said.

"You're robbing us?" I asked, but I knew what he was really after.

"Do what I said."

I reached into a pocket and showed him a handful of change.

"Now the other one," he commanded.

I took a deep breath and turned out the other pocket. The little brass bell fell into my hand and gleamed in the firelight.

"Here." He held out a hand. "Give it to me."

I handed it over.

"So you haven't found anything," he accused.

"That was lying on the sand," I said. "We looked all over this afternoon, but we couldn't find anything else. I think Absalom may have dropped it."

"You're lying," he said.

"I told you, it was on the sand. That doesn't tell anybody where the original grave is. It could be ten miles from here, on either side of the river."

"I don't believe you," he said.

"Look for yourself, then," I invited. "But meanwhile I'd like my boat back."

He glared at me from under an old baseball cap. "You better hope you get out of here alive."

"You're going to kill us?" I asked. "That wouldn't be very bright, would it? I mean, first T-Joe Dupont, then Absalom, and now two more. Are you going to kill the whole world?"

He thrust out his jaw. "I never killed nobody. All I ever done was run people like you off this land. Because it's our land, and my people are buried here."

"Then give us our boat and consider us run off," I said.

He sneered. "You're slick, real slick. That's the way they all were, when they got our land. Talk, always talk, just like a car salesman. Sign here, Chief. Oh, yeah, I know how that went."

"Well, I wasn't there when all that happened," I said.

"But I believe what you're saying, at least about how the land got taken. But just remember, when everybody else wanted to kill the Indians, the anthropologists were defending them."

"Defending?" He shook his head. "You call pulling up the bones of the old people defending? I've seen 'em in the displays. Like they was *things*, not real people."

"He's got a point," Pepper said, taking me by surprise. "But now there're laws and—"

"Laws—" Our captor spat again. "You just showed me how much the laws matter. You people are no different from that guard who dug up the first Tunica Treasure."

I folded my arms across my chest. "You still didn't answer my question, Ben. What are you planning to do with us?"

"I haven't made up my mind."

"Then it's going to be a long night."

"Be quiet! You're making me mad. You're just like some of the ones at the reservation, not interested in nothing but taking care of their own selves."

"The casino," I suggested.

"Hell yes," he snarled. "They didn't care a thing about the burials after all that."

"What do you mean?" Pepper asked, but I knew what he was going to say.

"The old chief, Chief Joe, let the archaeologists dig wherever they wanted," our captor said. "After he died, the new leaders wouldn't allow it. Now they've sold out, too. They didn't care if the developers put the casino on top of a burial ground on the reservation so long as the leaders made money."

"Is that true?" Pepper looked at me.

"There were two archaeological surveys," I said. "They didn't turn up any bones. That's all I know."

"They didn't look," Ben said.

"I wouldn't know about that," I said. "Except the firms involved have good reputations. They don't need to have an unlocated burial coming back at them."

"You're defending them," he said.

"No. Just trying to be logical."

"White man's logic," he said.

"I'm a white man," I told him. "A hungry one right now. You don't have anything to eat, do you?"

Ben Picote took a deep breath, then stepped back from the fire. He reached down and I saw what looked like an old schoolbag. He tossed me something wrapped in a bandanna. I unwrapped it and saw some cheese and a half-loaf of French bread.

"Thank you." I broke off a piece of the bread and handed it to Pepper. Then I gave her a piece of the cheese.

"Sit down," I invited him. "There's no need for you to stand up. It doesn't look like we're going anywhere."

He considered for a moment, then lowered himself slowly to a sitting position across from us.

"Don't try anything," he warned. "I've still got this gun."

"Twenty-two, isn't it?" I asked.

"A .222," he said. "So don't get any big ideas."

We ate in silence and when I'd finished I wiped my mouth. "Got any water?" I asked.

"You want a lot," he said and then tossed over a plastic canteen. I took a couple of swallows and passed it to Pepper. Then I flipped it back to him.

"So have you decided what you're going to do with us?" I asked.

"I don't know," he said. "I've got to think about it."

"Sure."

He took a quick sip of water, his black eyes never leaving us. "If I let you go, you're going to come back here, aren't you?"

"I don't know. Like I said, I don't think there's anything on this island."

"But you'll go on looking somewhere else."

"That's my job." I shrugged. "But I won't break the law. I won't dig up your peoples' bones."

"I don't believe you."

I stretched out my hands to the fire, hoping he couldn't see them shaking.

"That's your call, Ben. But it won't solve the problem if you kill us."

"I didn't say I was going to kill you," he said, changing the rifle from one hand to the other. "You're putting words in my mouth."

"I'm sorry." I shifted slightly. "Look, Ben, does your family know you're over here?"

"Never mind about my family. I take care of myself."

"And it's pretty clear you can. I just thought your dad or your mother . . ."

"I don't have a dad. He's been gone for five years. Killed in a wreck on Highway 1. My mama has other kids to take care of."

"Your brothers and sisters?"

His turn to shrug. "Two brothers, a sister. But that doesn't matter. What are you trying to do?" His face turned into a sneer. "Study the red man?"

"No. Just study Ben, maybe."

"Don't bother. All you gotta study is this rifle."

He lapsed into a sullen mood, the weapon resting across his knees, and I let myself relax. As I sat back slowly, I sensed some of the tension leaving Pepper. She flexed the hurt ankle and I knew she was telling me she could walk if she had to.

I told myself that we had the advantage, because he had to watch us and stay awake, while we could doze. He seemed to realize that, because several times in the next few hours he got up and pulled out a cigarette and walked back and forth to keep himself awake, but just before dawn I rolled over, and across the embers of the fire I saw that his eyes appeared to be closed.

Of course, he could be watching and waiting, but this was as good a chance as we'd ever get. I inched my hand over and nudged Pepper. She turned her head to me, our eyes met, and she slowly nodded.

I drew my feet up to me and then levered myself into a sitting position. I waited for him to awaken, but there was no reaction. Slowly, I pushed myself up to a squatting position, then stood. He was only a few feet away and if I reached for the gun I'd have a good chance of snagging it. But all I needed was for him to clamp a hand on the trigger guard and we'd be in a free-for-all. Two bodies rolling over on the sand were a prescription for somebody's getting shot, while if he caught us just trying to sneak away I didn't think he'd shoot.

I didn't think.

Pepper reached up and I caught her hand and pulled her upright. She grimaced and then shook her head, telling me she could make it. I nodded toward the head of the island and she gave a little shrug and followed, hopping after me across the sand. The cloud cover had dissipated now, and there was a milky moon, washing the island in a sickly white. The waves brushing the shore swallowed the sounds of our steps, and I thought we were going to make it when she stumbled, giving a little cry as she fell forward.

"Hey!" He was on his feet now and I couldn't think of anything else to do, so I ran back toward him, head down. My hands caught the barrel and drove the weapon to the side. He swore and tried to pull the gun away, but I pushed forward, pitting my weight against his own. He fell back and the gun flew out of his hand. I went down on top of him but his knee came up, catching me in the chest. I grunted and he rolled away, clawing for the rifle. I grabbed his feet and dragged him toward me and he swung the barrel toward my head. I parried with my arm and levered myself onto one knee. Years ago, when I was younger and lighter, I'd taken a few months of karate, and without thinking I gave him a punch to the head with my doubled fist. He went down then, falling on top of the rifle, and I took out after Pepper.

She was watching, horrified, from fifty yards away.

"Where are we going?" she asked, as I caught up, puffing.

"He has to have taken the boat someplace. Since he didn't pass us in it downstream, he must have dragged it upstream. But it's tough pulling a boat that big, so he can't have gone far."

I heard her exhale: "I hope you're right."

Fortunately, I was: Behind a fallen tree that served as a natural barrier, sloping down into the water at an angle, was the boat. I untied the painter and motioned for her to get in, then reached out for the paddle she extended and pulled so that the boat slowly came parallel to the shore. I stepped in and she shifted her weight to the other side. Now, ensconced at the stern, I turned my attention to the motor.

God, let him not have sabotaged it. Drifting down the Mississippi in a dawn mist without any power was not my idea of fun.

I yanked the cord and the engine started. I steered away from shore, hoping we could melt into the fog before he could get a bead on us. The boat chugged away from shore and into the current and I felt our forward progress slow. If we could just get away from the island long enough to steer back for the shore, where the current would be less . . .

There was sound behind us on the island, movement.

"Stop!" It was his voice and I ducked down, trying to make less of a target. "Come back here!"

I gritted my teeth, waiting. All he had to do was hit the motor and we'd come to a dead stop.

Pepper called out from the bow, but I couldn't make out the words. Then I understood, because the first bullet plopped into the water two feet from my face.

"I said," she yelled back, "*he's shooting*."

The rifle cracked again and water geysered up a foot from the bow.

I wrenched the tiller, steering back toward shore, then straightened out again, trying to make our movement too erratic for him to hold us in his sights, but all along I knew we were too slow for it to matter.

A third bullet sang over our heads and went off into the darkness.

He couldn't be that bad a shot, so why hadn't he hit us by now?

The fog had closed over us by the time I realized the answer: *He hadn't wanted to.*

I steered toward the bank, and the boat shuddered as it hit a submerged log. I grabbed the gunwale, felt the tremor pass. The shore loomed over us and I searched unsuccessfully for familiar features. What if we passed the launch site in the dark? How far would we have to go to find a spot to put in? What if we hit another snag, one that gutted the boat open like a tin can, dumping us into the treacherous waters? *What if . . . ?*

The bank gave way and ahead, as the mist parted, I saw a sloping surface and—yes—my Blazer. I nosed in and felt the prow of the boat bump into the mud of the shore. Pepper tumbled out and, painter in hand, tugged us up until I could make my way forward, get out, and help her pull the boat up to where I could attach the cable for the winch.

Ten minutes later, with the boat safely on the trailer, we sat in my vehicle, the windows rolled up against the predawn chill.

For a long time we remained motionless, but finally Pepper spoke.

"I just want to say I admire the way you kept your cool," she said. "I was impressed."

"Thank you," I said through chattering teeth.

TWENTY

A sleepy deputy took our report and we waited on a bench in the sheriff's office, half-dozing, until ten o'clock, when a deputy on the day shift came over and told us they'd found Absalom's body. Then he made me repeat Ben's description.

"Skinny, just under six feet, black hair, swarthy, black eyes, and a baseball cap," I told him. "But I don't think he did it."

The deputy grunted and waddled away. We went out for a late breakfast and when we got back a man from the D.A.'s office was waiting to talk to us. He was young, with curly, mussed hair, and looked like his last year in law school had left him frazzled. He kept asking about Ben, and why we didn't think he'd done it.

"People remember the Tunica Treasure," he said with a head shake. "They don't have a real kindly opinion about these Indians. Most people around here figure the guy that dug up the treasure had a right to it, not some tribe that hasn't lived here for two hundred years."

"You'd prosecute on that basis?" I asked.

"I'm just saying how people feel," he said. "Besides, this Ben fellow shot at you. You both said so. So why wouldn't he shoot the man you found?"

"Was Absalom Moon shot?" I asked.

The prosecutor frowned, obviously discomfited. "That's got to wait for the autopsy. But we know he shot Joseph Dupont."

"We do?"

The lawyer looked surprised. "The pathologist's report said he was shot with a .22 and you told me just now that's what this Ben carries."

"No, I said a .222. Same diameter bullet, but the .222 has a higher velocity."

"I know that, Mr. Graham. Believe it or not, I even own one. But whether the bullet goes fast enough to pass through a skull instead of stopping inside, like happened with Dupont, I'll leave to the medical people. Right now we'll settle for laying hands on this Ben."

At eleven-thirty we got permission to go home. I took Pepper back to the Dupont place to get her car. As we passed Greenbriar, I had the eerie sense of someone watching, but I realized it was probably excitement combined with lack of sleep. We drove back to Baton Rouge, and when we reached my office she pulled in, got out, and gave me a formal handshake.

"Thanks," she said.

"For what? I almost got you killed."

"I think it was the other way around. Going out there again was my idea, remember?"

I rubbed my eyes. "I'm not sure I remember anything right now."

I watched her get into the Integra and then went inside to report to Marilyn. I'd called her from the sheriff's office, but she was still upset. There was a message slip from the State Archaeologist on my desk, but I ignored it, calling David, instead. I gave him a brief report and accepted his reprimand.

"Christ, man, you don't go out on that river in a little boat no matter who the woman is."

"You're right," I said. Then I hung up and called Willie Dupont. He listened while I told him about our visit to the island and escape.

"You don't think the kid killed my dad?"

"No."

"Why not? He's got reason. And he may have the right gun."

"Yeah," I said. "But everybody in the world's got some kind of .22, don't they?"

"Sure. I got a couple. So what's the real reason?"

"He could've killed us and he didn't."

"Maybe him and Dad got in a argument. People do things when they're mad."

"Like kill their fathers?"

"What?"

"Your sister called us. She says you were burned because your father bought the property in the first place, that you pitched a fit in front of Carter Wascom."

Willie breathed out. "Dominique. I should've known it. Probably told you to stop what you're doing. My sister's a bitch."

"She said she had the power of attorney nullified."

"She did. But I got my own lawyer. I'll fight her every step."

"Why were you against the purchase?"

"Sometimes Dad thought he was still in the glory days, when oil was forty-five dollars a barrel. I thought the land was overpriced. And I was still resentful. Hell yes, I'll admit it: He wouldn't pay five hundred bucks to bail me out of jail but he could spend half a million for a place to go on weekends."

"But you changed your mind."

"I grew up. When I saw my father dead I realized what an asshole I'd been. But now I'll never have a chance to tell him. That's the part hurts."

"Yeah."

I told him goodbye and called Chloe Messner.

"Tooth? Oh, that one. Well, I'm not supposed to comment on ongoing investigations but seeing as how you got me into this, I guess I can say that the tooth is definitely not from Joseph Dupont's mouth."

"I'd figured that out."

"The filling is a material that hasn't been used for twenty or thirty years. The tooth is yellowed, completely different wear pattern than Joseph Dupont's premolars. I think it's been lying around somewhere for a long time."

"Like in a grave?"

"Very possibly."

I thanked her and went home. I fed a grateful Digger, showered, and then fell into bed.

I should have slept, but for a long time images of the river kept swirling through my head. I was in a whirlpool, spinning around, and every time I passed the shore I reached out for help. But the only person on the shore was Carter Wascom and he was staring down at me with a perplexed look, as if he couldn't make up his mind.

When I opened my eyes it was dark outside. I tried to move but I felt drugged. Finally, the heaviness of sleep fell away and I sat up on the side of the bed. Digger was nuzzling my leg, telling me he was ready for his supper.

I fed him and, resigned, took out a TV dinner for myself. I'd already fixed a glass of iced tea when it occurred to me to check my answering machine in the study. Sure enough, the red light was blinking.

"Alan, I'm calling at five-eighteen on Friday." I went on alert: It was Pepper's voice. *"Your secretary said you were at home. I came by, but nobody answered the door . . ."* Hesitation. *"Give me a call, will you? I'll be at home . . ."* She gave her number and I fumbled for a pencil to write it down. *"I just heard on the news: They caught Ben."*

I was still standing by the phone, trying to digest the information, when I heard Digger barking. I went out to the living room and saw a blurred form through the opaque glass of the front door. Too big for a woman, so who could it be?

I slid back the dead bolt and edged the door open.

"Freddie," I said, nonplussed.

"Alan." Freddie St. Ambrose beamed back at me from the front porch, his round face all smiles. "I hope I'm not bothering you, but I thought I'd drop by on the way home. Working a little late tonight, you know."

"Of course." I swung the door open and stood aside. I'd known Freddie for eight or nine years but the closest we'd ever been socially was my turning down his offer of a drink at the country club when he'd had some particularly slimy scheme to propose.

"Thank you." He danced in, surprisingly light on his feet for a man of his girth. I took in the silk tie, blazer, and lizard-skin shoes.

"Nice costume," I said.

"Now, Alan, that's no way to greet a guest." He laid his umbrella in the corner, then eyed my living room. "Nice home you have, Al. I've heard about it, and I'm glad to finally get to see it. Your family digs, right? Nice. Very nice. A little like a museum, but . . ." He shrugged. "To each his own, I always say."

"What's on your mind, Freddie?"

"May I sit down?" He reached down, felt the sofa, and took a seat. Digger advanced on him with a growl. "That goddamn dog better not bite," he warned.

"He won't," I said. "Unless I tell him, or you keep cussing him."

Freddie gulped and rubbed a hand over his dark beard. "I should tell you I'm allergic to animals."

"Digger's allergic to some humans. Look, Freddie, say your piece. And I better tell you right now, I know you called Ghecko and tried to stir him up about our project."

Freddie drew back, offended. "Al, I did no such thing and I very much resent the implication. You know how Ghecko is, always scared of his shadow. Actually"—he leaned forward now—"it's sort of about that I came here tonight."

"About what?"

"Ghecko. And your new friend."

"My friend?"

"That woman, for God's sake, do I have to spell it all out?"

I sat down across from him. "What about her?"

"She's trouble, Al. Like I've been trying to tell you from the first. We really need to stand together on this."

"My supper's waiting, Freddie."

He sniffed. "Yes, I thought I smelled something burning. Look, I'm trying to tell you, Al: she's doing a double-cross."

I felt my skin tingle.

"How do you figure that?" I demanded.

"I thought I'd get your attention. Listen, Al, you and she, you aren't, well . . . ?" He made a crude gesture with his finger and fist.

"Get on with it, or I'll call the dog."

"All right, all right." He sat up straight, looking put upon. "Did you know she'd called Ghecko today to talk about getting an archaeological permit?"

"For where?"

"Are you sure you want to know? You haven't been very collegial lately."

I stared back at him, then I looked over at Digger, lying in the hallway with his muzzle on his paws.

Freddie sighed. "Angola. She wants to do a survey at Angola."

"The prison?"

"None other."

"It's already been studied," I said. "Ford, Kniffen, Haag, the work at Bloodhound Hill . . ."

"But not a complete survey, Al. Those were just known sites. She wants to try to locate historic Tunica sites that haven't been found yet."

The tingling spread.

"That's no crime," I said. "Besides, the state prison isn't going to give anybody permission. They're still hostile up there because the original treasure was found by one of their guards and they figure he got screwed out of it."

"Before now, that was the case. But there's a new warden, Levi Goodeau. Bit of a liberal. She's already called him and he thinks it's a good idea. She's also talked to the Tunicas."

"*What*?" My voice sounded shrill even to me.

"That's right." Freddie rubbed his plump hands together. "And she's done a little digging in the archives. Land records, you know?"

"Land records?"

"Sure. At the State Land Office on Third Street. Doesn't take long. You mean she hasn't told you about this?"

"You mean she's told *you*?" I countered.

"Of course not. She talked to Ghecko, laid it all out for him. I just happened to go to lunch with him today and he babbled, as we both know he's inclined to do."

I could see it now, Ghecko wringing his hands and explaining to a grave-faced Freddie that he had misgivings, but that, as State Archaeologist, he couldn't play favorites, no cause to deny her a permit, etc. Then, having thought it over, the Echo had called me to spill the same news so I wouldn't get mad if I heard it from Freddie first. Only I hadn't returned his call . . .

I took a deep breath. "Well, she and I aren't partners. She has a right to do her own research."

"Of *course* she does. Free country and all that. That's what I like about you, Al: You're such an idealist. You'll still be talking about intellectual freedom when you're sitting on the curb, begging for handouts."

"Get out of here, Freddie."

The fat man rose slowly. "I just hope you remember I was the one who brought this to your attention. And that I was also the one who proposed that we nip this thing in the bud at the very first."

"I'll remember," I said, opening the door for him.

He turned to consider the room a final time. "You know, Al, you really do have some nice furniture here. That Queen Anne sofa, for instance. I bet you don't even know what it's worth. If you ever get short of money, I'll take it off your hands. Top dollar. Might even bid on the house and furnishings *in toto*."

"Don't call me Al," I said, and shut the door after him.

Digger gave a growl of good riddance and I reached down and scratched him between the ears. "I know, fella. He hits me the same way."

I went back to the study and stared down at the number I'd scribbled on my pad. Was Freddie telling the truth? Was Pepper in the process of pulling a double-cross, lining up a project that would capitalize on whatever she found as part of her work with me? Had I been a sucker to listen to her at all? I hesitated, then punched in the number and waited. After two rings I heard her voice.

"It's me," I said.

"Alan. Are you all right?"

"Fine. I've been asleep." *And you*, I thought, *have prob-*

*ably been down to Ghecko's again, sweet-talking the poor
bastard.*

"Look, you got the message about Ben? They caught
him. He's in jail in St. Francisville."

"You heard this on the news?"

"Yes. I caught a television flash. Alan, is everything all
right? Your voice sounds funny."

"Where are you?"

There was the briefest hesitation.

"I'm at home."

"We need to talk."

"Isn't that what we're doing?"

"I like to look somebody in the eye when I talk to
them."

"That's old-fashioned of you. Look, if there's something
the matter, I wish you'd tell me."

"I think we ought to meet," I said. "Name a place."

A sigh. "This *does* sound serious. Well, I guess I could
come to your place. Or we could meet at my office."

"What about your place?"

More hesitation. "Oh, well, I don't know . . ."

"Give me the address. That way you won't have to set
foot out."

"That's not a problem. Really, I mean, there's no need—"

"The address?"

When she spoke again her voice was almost too low to
be heard. "I'm in University Acres. Really, Alan, we could
go to your office, it's closer for both of us and—"

"What Street?"

"Oxford."

"Number?"

She gave a number, then: "You'll have to go behind the
house. It's an apartment."

"I'll find it."

It took ten minutes to get there. It was one of the city's
oldest subdivisions, located on the south side of the university on what used to one of the plantations that stretched
along an old route called the Highland Road, and which

was now one of the city's main thoroughfares.

Lots of my schoolmates had lived in this subdivision and even Sam MacGregor had lived here in the days when he'd taught me my first anthropology courses. Despite new cars in the driveways, it still struck me as a sleepy place, with spreading oaks and sedate old homes built for professors and lawyers.

I found the address without any trouble. It was a 1930s-style bungalow with brick pillars, a screened-in front porch, and a Dodge Caravan in the driveway. I stopped at the curb and got out. She'd said behind the house.

I looked down the drive and saw the garage with a second story and a flight of steps leading up.

My God, no wonder she'd been hesitant. *The immaculately dressed P. E. Courtney lived in a garage apartment.*

I hesitated, then started past the van. When I got to the foot of the steps I saw her standing at the top, looking down. This time there were no designer jeans, just a pair of faded cutoffs and a T-shirt.

All at once I felt out of place, like I'd caught her on the examining table in her doctor's office.

"Hi," she said as I reached the top. She held out a hand and I took it, surprised at how small it suddenly seemed.

"Look," I said. "I was just trying to save you trouble. I . . ."

"Doesn't matter." She shrugged and opened a screen door. "You're here now. Anyway, why should it matter?"

She held the door for me and I walked into a tiny living room with oak floorboards and an acoustic tile ceiling. There was a metal bookcase in one corner and a small TV on a crate against one wall. A couple of cardboard boxes showed that she hadn't finished unpacking.

"Sit down." She pointed to a sofa with a blanket over it to cover the holes. "Can I offer you something to drink? Tea or coffee?"

"No. Thanks." I sat down and felt the springs give.

"You expected something a little more upscale," she said. "Well, I had to make a decision about where to put my money. I decided it was better to have an office and a decent-looking car. After all, you don't usually take your clients home.''

"No," I said.

"A physics professor rents this to me," she said. "He has a couple of kids. Nice kids, actually. And it isn't so much different from what I've been used to as a graduate student."

I nodded, trying to get my thoughts together. All at once my anger at her melted away.

"But something's bothering you," she said, sitting down across from me in a canvas basket chair. "Or you wouldn't have come here."

"You've been trying to get a permit from Ghecko," I blurted. "You've been trying to put together some kind of deal to do work at Angola and probably some other places."

Her brows edged up fractionally. For the first time I realized she wasn't wearing her glasses.

"That's true. I told you I was interested in the contact period. I thought if I could get into Angola there might be some clues about where the Tunica were before and after they went to the Trudeau site. I called Warden Goodeau and he sounded interested. So I went down to the State Land Office and looked at the old ownership maps."

"You did this without telling anybody?"

"You mean without telling *you*? This was the other day. We weren't exactly on the best terms, remember? But, for the record, if you were going to cut me in on the Dupont survey, I was going to cut you in on whatever I found."

"But in the meantime, if I had to do additional work to back up any of the finds at T-Joe's, I'd be running smack up against your permit to work on Angola and the surrounding area."

"Well . . ."

"By the way, does the *surrounding area* include the Trudeau site, where they found the original Tunica Treasure?"

Her eyes dropped. "They said they wouldn't give anybody a permit for that site because it was too sensitive."

"An understatement." I got up, my anger returning. "So you were going to box me in. Get access to any collections from the area covered by your permit and keep me from using them until you were finished, which means long enough to keep me from finishing my report to T-Joe."

"Alan, it wasn't like that. I wanted you to let me work with you searching for the lost village. That's all. I didn't even want more than a polite acknowledgment. I just didn't want to be left out in the cold when another discovery like the Tunica Treasure was made. I wanted to be there." She gave a tiny shrug. "The permit was just a kind of insurance policy."

"And to think I was starting to trust you."

Her eyes met my own. "And you still can. Look, I hadn't written up the proposal for the Angola work. I was just exploring what was possible. But you can go with me tomorrow to talk to Goodeau. I'll tell him we're going to work together. Will that make you feel better?"

"You have an appointment with Goodeau tomorrow?"

"Yes. I made it the day before yesterday. He was very obliging. He said he was working all Saturday and he'd be glad to see me."

"I see. But if I hadn't found out about this, you'd still be meeting him alone."

"I realized afterward I ought to tell you. I just never got up the nerve."

It was my turn to look surprised. "You? A lack of nerve?"

"I can understand if you're mad. But I wanted to be a part of the project . . ." She let out her breath slowly. "Look, I'll back off. I'll call Goodeau and tell him I've changed my mind. You're a good archaeologist and a good person, and I don't want to screw you up."

My anger started to melt, despite my suspicion that she was taking me for a sucker.

"And you're a good archaeologist, too," I heard myself say. "At least, a good archaeologist wrote the Polhugh report. It's just that . . ."

"I know. I push too much."

"You said it."

She nodded. "So I'll tell Goodeau never mind."

"Now hold up on that." My mouth had run away with me again.

"But . . ." I saw the hope in her eyes. Without the glasses she looked almost approachable.

"Maybe we can work something out," I conceded. "It's been years since anybody was allowed to work at Angola. I'd hate to see the chance lost."

"We can work together," she said. "All we need is funding."

"Is that all?"

"Don't look so cynical. The State Archaeologist said they have some money left in their grant fund, if we can find a match, and the warden said he knew people who might put up some money."

"Okay," I said, sighing. "We'll work together."

"You won't be sorry."

I didn't answer, just got up slowly. "What time tomorrow?"

"The appointment's at ten."

"I'll pick you up at eight-thirty," I said.

She shook her head. "I'll pick *you* up."

I started to say something, then held my tongue.

"Okay," I said. "At my office."

She nodded and followed me to the door. "Take care," she said and I nodded, standing on the landing for a second in the night air. A little voice told me I was being a damn fool.

TWENTY-ONE

The morning newspaper gave the story of the capture. Ben Picote, seventeen, of Marksville, had been captured by sheriff's deputies only a hundred yards or so from where we'd left him. Ballistics tests were being made on his rifle and an autopsy was being planned on the body of Absalom Moon. Moon's body had been found, according to the story, by a pair of hunters. Since it wasn't hunting season, I wondered who had written the story. It didn't matter, though, because they'd kept us out of it, mainly, I suspected, because we'd been gone by the time the story had been put together. There was no mention of a treasure or, indeed, of any motive, other than the suggestion that Ben had been caught trespassing. I tore out the article and stuck it in my pocket. Then I fed Digger, ate a couple of pieces of cheese toast, and drove to the office.

Marilyn's wrath was untamable.

"You didn't come in at all yesterday and now you're taking off again with that woman?" she fumed. "I had to forge your name to all the paychecks. I'm working Saturdays because I don't have enough help in the office and you have crew working overtime because of the Corps deadline, which means time and a half we can't pay, and if another check from the Corps doesn't come in soon there won't be another payday no matter *who* signs."

I nodded absently, having heard it all before.

"Maybe a check'll be at the box today," I said.

David hobbled in then, his leg in a cast, and Marilyn flew to his side for help.

"Alan's going off with that woman."

David blinked and lurched against the sorting table.

"Is this serious?" he asked. "Or just a one-nighter?"

Gator grinned. "He's already had one night. Now he's going for the whole month."

"That's enough," I said. Then I told them about our appointment with Warden Goodeau. "There's the chance of getting another project. Besides, it's the only way to keep her from blocking us if we run into anything that requires further work."

Marilyn, ever jealous of her position and fearful of interlopers, snarled a one-syllable word that rhymed with *witch*.

David, as usual, applied logic.

"You know the Tunicas would raise hell if anybody did any work at Angola or Trudeau," he said. "Anything anybody finds is likely to be grave goods and the law says—"

"The Tunicas are all wrapped up in their new casino," I said. "And Ghecko sounds like he'll allow the permit to go through. You want to be here sitting on your ass while somebody else does the work up there? Remember, there're Indian mounds a thousand years old right outside the prison gates. They don't have anything to do with the Tunica. And there was a Poverty Point site three thousand years old where the prison hospital is right now. Who the hell knows what else is out there?"

David nodded. "That's true enough."

Marilyn spun on her heel. "Remind me to say *I told you so* when that woman stabs you in the back."

I shrugged, then went into my office and signed paychecks, and when I glanced up *that woman* was standing in my doorway, looking the same, with the designer glasses and Liz Claiborne clothes, as she had the day I'd met her.

"I don't think your secretary likes me," she said.

"Let's go," I told her, hoping to get out before Marilyn sent something sailing at both our heads.

*　　*　　*

It took exactly an hour to reach the prison gates. In the old days, there'd been twenty miles of winding two-lane from U.S. 61, north of St. Francisville, with the bramble overgrown loess hills looming on either side. In recent years the road had been broadened, with the worst curves of the old road straightened out. The parish had lost something, I thought, replacing atmosphere with business.

A mile before the end of the road is the community of Tunica, and beyond it, overlooking the river, is the spot where the original Tunica Treasure was found. The road swings right at Tunica, arrowing between the river at the base of the hills, and the old railroad bed on the right. Once, this had been the domain of the Tunicas, who had been pushed south from their original home in Mississippi. But before them, there had been other tribes, most long lost in the mists of history. The Tunicas and their treasure was a great story, but there were other stories here that could also stand telling, if only we had the data.

We slowed at the prison entrance and a guard lumbered out of the gatehouse and asked our business. When Pepper told him it was to meet the warden the guard seemed unimpressed and told us to get out so the car could be searched. Afterward, he gave us plastic visitors' badges and told us to drive over to the green administration building.

We parked, got out, and locked the car.

"This is the first time I've been in a prison," Pepper said, looking around her. A trustee in white T-shirt and dungarees was busy in the garden beside the green building, and in the distance a couple of guards on horseback watched a column of inmates headed for the fields.

"It's not a fun place," I said, thinking of what I'd read about the prison's history. In the early fifties, some convicts had gotten so desperate they'd caused a national scandal by cutting their Achilles tendons. Things had never been that bad since, but the sprawling penal farm, a miasmal stretch of river mud stuck between the Mississippi and the hills, would never be a pleasant place.

We went to the front door and a trustee opened it for us. A guard in the corridor told us the warden's office was at the end.

"God," Pepper said, shuddering, "I keep expecting to pass one of these rooms and see the electric chair inside."

"Nah. They use a needle now," I said.

We came to the end, where a bulletin board graced the flaking green wall. The board was filled with Civil Service fliers and notices of hearings on various subjects, from increasing the number of law books in the prison library to a grievance about the quality of food.

I opened the door of the reception room and followed Pepper in.

The receptionist, a middle-aged woman with garish red hair, looked up from a computer screen.

"Yes?"

Pepper handed over her business card and the woman reached down for the glasses that hung from her neck on a black ribbon.

"Dr. Courtney," she said. "Yes." She swiveled on her chair and peered in my direction. "And this is . . . ?"

"Dr. Graham," Pepper said. "The warden knows him."

"Does he?" the woman said, unimpressed. "Well, Warden Goodeau is on the farm right now. You can wait there . . ." She nodded at a couch and some straight-backed chairs. "He ought to be back in a little while."

Pepper and I exchanged looks.

"All right," Pepper said and sat down. I took a seat in one of the chairs.

I looked out the window and tried to imagine what it would be like to spend ten or fifteen years in the fields under the eyes of the men on horses.

I was still wondering at ten-thirty when the door opened and Levi Goodeau stepped in, removing his straw hat.

"Sorry to be late," he said, smiling at Pepper. "We had a little problem out at Camp J."

The secretary handed him a message slip.

"A call from the governor's office," she said.

Goodeau scanned the pink piece of paper. "I'll take care of it." He stuffed it in his shirt pocket and motioned us toward a door at the rear of the room. "Come on into my office."

Pepper went after him and I followed. The warden's office was a step up from the drab surroundings outside, with paneled walls and some framed photographs of Goodeau with politicians. I recognized the governor, one of the state's two senators, and, oddly, a photo of the warden in work clothes alongside a similarly clad Jimmy Carter.

"Habitat for Humanity," Goodeau said, nodding at the picture. "I gave a couple of weeks a few years back, when I was on the faculty of the university. President Carter was one of the people I met. Nice man."

"You're a sociologist," I said, taking a seat in one of the cushioned chairs.

"That's right," Goodeau said. "Came from Tunica, right down the road. I was in prison administration for a few years and then I got my doctorate at LSU. Did a lot of consulting for Corrections. They tolerated me because I was a home boy, but when the governor picked me for warden here, the stuff nearly hit the fan. The old-timers thought I was just a do-gooder. Said I couldn't ever keep things from falling apart."

"Old-timers like young Brincy," I suggested.

He nodded. "He's one. But there're lots like him. Grew up as part of this system and can't stand to see anything change. I can deal with Briney because his father and I are old fishing buddies. But some of the others . . ." He shook his head.

"It must be a hard job," Pepper said.

Goodeau smiled. "It's not easy. This place has a reputation as one of the hardest prisons in the country. What we get here are the worst the state has to offer—the first offenders, the embezzlers, and the drug cases mostly go to one of the other prisons. We, we get the lifers, or the ones with twenty years, or . . ." He sighed. "The ones with death sentences."

"But you think you can make a difference," I said.

The warden shrugged. "I have to tell myself that. You see ever since this place became a state penitentiary, around the turn of the century, the warden's been a boss. It's a throwback to the days when this was a plantation that rented inmates from the state. The overseer was the boss back then. Hundreds died under that system, so the state bought the land and made it into a public institution. But the same practices continued. They even armed some of the inmates, the trustees, and made them guards over the others. It was supposed to save money. And that was pretty much the way it was, except for a couple of deviations.'' He got up from his chair, no longer the warden, but the professor delivering a lecture. "Back in the early thirties they hired a man from Pennsylvania, a reformer. He caught a lot of flak for being too lenient. Then, one Sunday, eleven of the inmates staged a big break while the guards and their families were having a baseball game. Killed the guard captain and two others. Turned out the guns for the break had been smuggled in by a woman visiting a prisoner. The warden— they called him the prison manager then—caught hell. They claimed he'd revoked the order to search women visitors.''

Goodeau strode over to the window and looked out, hands clasped behind him. "They sent him packing, of course. Things pretty much stayed the same until the early fifties and the heel cuttings." He turned around to face us: "Things improved after that, and nowadays we don't have the cane fields, and inmates don't disappear, but it's still just a six-thousand-acre campground where you store people. And there're more coming every day."

He relapsed back into his chair as if all the hope had leaked out of him. "And fool that I am, I keep telling myself there has to be some better way for society to solve its problems than by sending men off for ten or twenty years or life. You see, even for those who don't have a life sentence, it can just as easily become one."

"Inmate killings?" Pepper asked.

"Oh, there're those, all right, though we're pretty good at keeping a lid on them. No, I mean AIDS. The day's coming when a man who comes here for five years will have a death sentence. It's spreading and nobody really cares. Society doesn't worry about a bunch of inmates." He stretched his hands out before him on the desk.

"I hadn't thought about that," Pepper said, shaking her head.

The warden nodded grimly. "Well, maybe we'll get

some help out of the legislature, right? At least, you have to try. Now, on to a more pleasant subject, this project of yours . . .''

"We think it would make a real contribution," Pepper blurted.

Goodeau nodded amiably. "I'm sure. I've done a little reading about this area. You know, I've always been interested in history. Sort of runs in the family, you might say."

"You've got about a thousand years of history right here," I said, and told him about the Tunica cemetery at Bloodhound Hill, inside the prison, and the even earlier Indian mounds throughout the area. He listened attentively, nodding and making approving sounds.

"And I suppose if you find anything else that relates to the Tunica, they'll want to claim the prison." He gave a nervous little chuckle.

"Always possible," I said. "But I don't think they're likely to get Angola."

"Just my cousin's plantation, eh?" Goodeau joked.

"Oh?" Pepper gave me a look.

"Well, not many people know it," the warden said, "but in the early part of the century, before our family bought it, the Indians made a claim to the place. Didn't get anywhere."

I sat forward in my chair: "This is in the records?"

"No. It was in an old diary my cousin Carter has. It was left in the house by the family that had it before the Civil War. Nobody paid any attention to it, but Eulalia found it and I think she was going to try to have it published when she got sick."

"Was this claim ever brought to court?"

"Well . . ." Goodeau's answer was cut short by a pounding on his door. He blinked.

"What is it?"

In answer, the door burst open and young Briney stood staring from one of us to the other.

"What's this about?" the warden demanded. "What do you mean breaking in like this?"

"It's about the chase team," Briney tried to explain. "The sheriff's asked us to help him."

"What?"

The phone in the outer office rang then and I heard the secretary saying something in a low voice.

"What's he need the chase team for?" Goodeau asked. His phone buzzed and he picked it up.

"Yes? Oh, hello, Sheriff." He listened, face intent, then nodded. "Sure. Any way we can." He replaced the receiver and gave Briney a sour look.

"That was the sheriff. Well, I gave him the chase team." He waved a hand, dismissing his subordinate, and then turned to us.

"Hell of a thing." He got up again and stuck his straw hat down on his bald dome.

"That Indian boy they locked up for killing old Absalom? He broke out of the jail and stole a boat. They want to use our hounds to run him down."

TWENTY-TWO

It was a long time before I could get my breath back.

"Escaped?" I heard Pepper's voice, as incredulous as I felt.

The warden started out, then stopped. "Look, I hope you'll excuse me. But I like to keep an eye on the guys when they go off on these chases. They can get carried away."

I mumbled something about understanding and we trailed after him, past the secretary's desk. The warden stopped abruptly:

"Mrs. Burr, if that investigator comes, tell him we'll just have to reschedule. I don't want him rummaging through my files if I'm not here."

Mrs. Burr nodded primly. "He won't get anywhere with me, Warden."

Goodeau glanced back over his shoulder. "Never a day without a crisis," he tried to joke.

We watched him go and I saw Mrs. Burr give an almost imperceptible shake of her head.

"It's a lot of stress to be under, being a warden," I said.

Mrs. Burr looked up quickly. "Stress? You don't know the half of it. Such a good man. You know, I worked for Warden Goodeau when he was at the university. I wouldn't have come up here for anybody else. He tries so hard to protect his people, but you know what they have here . . ." She leaned toward us. "Just a bunch of good old boy types."

181

I thought of young Briney and couldn't find anything to say in contradiction.

"Then there's stress from on top," she went on. "All the politicians want favors. A job for somebody, special treatment for somebody's brother-in-law who's here for ninety-nine years for a double murder. And now the State Attorney General, trying to uncover brutality." She tsked and brought herself up straight in the chair. "Well, what do they expect? It's a brutal place. Everyone who works here is brutal, except for a few of the social workers and Warden Goodeau. But I keep asking him, how long can anyone keep working here and not become brutal, too?"

We left her at the desk and as we rounded a corner in the corridor almost collided with a young man with shined shoes and a briefcase that spelled lawyer. The AG's man, I thought. Poor Warden Goodeau.

We were out the gate before either of us spoke to the other.

"They'll kill him," she said. "I can feel it."

I remembered the posse that had found us on the island. She was right. And if they didn't, the deputies would.

"He shouldn't have run," I said.

She turned on me, eyes flashing: "Why not? If you're not guilty, why just stand there and take it? His people have been doing that for hundreds of years. What has it gotten them?"

"I know. Still, it wasn't smart. If he'd stayed put a lawyer could have gotten him off."

"You think so." We were passing through Tunica now and I saw a man in prison blue, with sideburns and a leather-tanned face, talking to someone outside the general store. She jerked her head in his direction. "You think a jury of *those* would vote for an Indian."

"Whoa. That's kind of harsh."

"Why? They hate blacks, don't they?"

"They aren't known for their liberal views," I conceded. "But Indians—"

"The Tunicas stirred up a lot of trouble when they claimed the original treasure," she said. "I read about it in Jeff Brain's book. People resented the fact that the Indians

ended up with something that had been found by a local
man, on private property the Indians hadn't been on for a
hundred and fifty years. So you think they wouldn't like to
get back at an Indian, and a Tunica at that?''

"I think you're being unreasonable," I said. "Besides,
the Indians have been making some ridiculous demands.''

"Oh?''

"Yes. They're suing to claim all of Marksville just because their reservation is there.''

"It makes more sense than anybody's wanting to live in
Marksville now," she declared.

"Have you ever *been* to Marksville?''

"Well, not exactly . . .''

"A very charming little town, for your information.
Classically French.''

"Founded by an Italian," she shot back.

"How did you know that?''

"I read, too. As a matter of fact, it was in one of your
own culture history reports in the state office.''

I folded my arms. "It doesn't matter. The point is that
the Indians are making some impossible demands.''

She gave me a sweet smile. "I'm sure some of your best
friends are Native Americans.''

"Well, they *are*.''

"God help us.''

"Just because I don't want to hand back every burial
archaeologists have recovered for the past two hundred
years," I complained. "My God, what kind of sense does
that make? The Tunica can't make any rational connection
to most of those burials, anyway. They're always ranting
about blood brotherhood, but the truth is that before the
whites came, all these tribes were at war with one another,
and it didn't stop after that. Both before and after the Europeans, they moved all over the place, not just small family
groups, but whole tribes. So how can a twentieth-century
Tunica or Sioux claim any kind of connection with some
burial from Wisconsin or Louisiana that dates from three
thousand B.C.? It probably wasn't even a member of their
group. *Their* group was probably the damn enemy.''

"You have the sensitivity of a slug," she said, and

stomped the accelerator. "No wonder the Native Americans want a little autonomy."

"Oh, I'm to blame for the whole business, just because I'm not politically correct?"

"You and people like you, yes. It was people like you who displayed Indian burials in museum cases with clever captions. Or who just stuck the bones away in the museum and never even analyzed them."

"This is incredible," I said. "Who did you say was your major professor? Angela Davis?"

"Who?"

It was my turn to utter God's name.

"Anyway," she said, "he'd end up with a public defender and you know how incompetent they are."

"So he won't get Johnnie Cochran," I admitted. "But they still have to have a certain amount of evidence. If they convict on less, the appeals court will throw it out."

"Are you willing to bet his life on that?" she asked quietly.

"I dunno."

"You know he's innocent."

"We agree on something. But I don't know if we agree for the same reasons."

"I'd like to hear yours."

I exhaled. "I've said them already: Ben's a youngster. Hot-blooded and full of resentment. But he didn't kill us when he had the chance. It was a real dilemma for him. He could have killed Absalom in the heat of the moment, if Absalom was in the middle of rifling a grave, sure. But he said he didn't and I believe him. I think, with all his blood up and his Indian pride, he'd have said so if he'd done it. Now what's *your* reasoning?"

"Elementary," she sniffed. "Ben gave himself too many motives for killing the old man to have really done it. A guilty person would never have admitted as much as Ben did. Besides, I don't think Ben knows where the burial ground is."

"No?"

"No. I think he was out there looking, just like we were. But if he'd found Absalom actually pilfering a grave, then there'd have been no need to keep looking."

"Interesting reasoning," I said, glancing back over my shoulder at the highway. "Anything else, before we get run over?"

"He didn't have a killer's eyes," she said in a near undertone.

"Oh."

She eased off the brake and we started forward again. I was thinking of the night on the river and the bullets zinging past my head. Was I right in my analysis? Had Ben missed on purpose, or was he just a lousy shot?

She turned to face me again: "Alan, we can't just let them murder him."

The car edged toward one of the bluffs on the side of the road and I took a deep breath.

"Oh? What are we going to do?"

She jerked the wheel just in time to keep from leaving the roadway.

"All I can think to do," she said, "is stop them."

My turn to look incredulous. "Stop them?"

"Yes. We've got to keep them from getting to him."

"Oh, I see. Well, how are we supposed to do that?"

"It's simple. We have to find him first. We have to go back to the island."

TWENTY-THREE

This time we went overland, like we had the first time, taking the trail behind Absalom Moon's house. We'd made a quick run back to Baton Rouge and I'd changed clothes, filled a couple of canteens, and picked up the Blazer. Marilyn and David, feverishly working on a draft report that was due on Monday, were horrified but I told them the search for Ben Picote was concentrated on the other side of the river, because a boat was missing and the law would figure he was headed for Marksville, his home.

"But you figure he'll be on the island," David said.

"I think there's a good chance. He figures his people are buried there and he has some romantic notion."

"Last of the Mohicans," Gator said, grinning like a jack o'lantern. "Look, boss, I'd feel better going."

"Thanks but no," I told him. "He at least knows the two of us. I bring a third and he may figure we've turned him in."

David consulted his watch. "I'll give you twenty-four hours," he said. "After that, it's the hounds."

"Fair enough," I said.

I sensed Marilyn's eyes burning a hole through my back, no doubt willing some misfortune to "that woman."

So now "that woman" and I were back where it had all started, only better provisioned, headed into the forest and toward a rendezvous that I hoped would save a life.

Stupid me.

It was easy enough to follow our trail to the point where

the track led into the gully. After that, it was a matter of sliding down the clay banks again with the eerie memory of how we'd been pursued. I kept looking back over my shoulder, half-expecting to see a shadow on the banks above, but there was nothing. It was far harder just to keep in front and finally I had to agree to let her take point, at the cost of some male pride.

But twenty minutes after entering the creek bed we came to the place where we'd slithered out before and clambered up onto the banks. A short stint on a west compass bearing brought us to the edge of the ridge and left us looking out over the floodplain below.

I lowered my pack to the ground and stretched. I was used to carrying equipment in the field, but this time I had more than the usual load: a jungle hammock in case we got stuck overnight, and a battery lantern. I looked over at Pepper, serene under her own knapsack. She was carrying her own hammock, flashlight, and food, but, by God, she was years younger than I was. It was a galling thought.

As if reading my mind, she gave me a sweet smile and gestured to the jungle below: "Shall we?"

And so we did.

I would like to say that I managed the feat upright and saved her a few broken bones, but the facts are otherwise. I did most of the hillside on my seat, and at one point, at least, was in danger of becoming a human landslide. It was, to be honest, the heavier pack, and I reminded myself as I watched her pick her way down like a mountain goat that she was carrying far less than I was.

Now, on the floor of the forest, with the fresh-ozone smell of the pines replaced by the stink of decayed vegetation, the only thing between us and the island was the swamp.

I got up, dusted myself off, and reached for my canteen. Then I saw her eyes on me and decided against it: If she didn't need a damn drink, neither did I.

"Would you like to go first?" she asked, and I sensed that it was a concession to my male ego.

"Ladies first," I insisted and made a Musketeer sweep with my baseball cap. There was still a chance she'd walk into a hole in the swamp and I'd have to pull her out.

She grinned and stepped out in front. I followed ten steps behind.

When we reached the edge of the swamp, she pulled out her compass and waited for the needle to stop.

"That way," she said finally. "West by northwest."

I checked my own compass. "I agree."

She stepped into the algae-covered water and I waited a few seconds, then followed.

We'd crossed this stretch before, of course, but it was impossible to say just where. In the dim light, with the leaning cypress and willows, everything looked alike.

I watched the water go up to her waist.

"I'd steer right," I said.

"I'm okay," she said back over her shoulder, and then plunged downward. But at the last second she reached out with her left hand, grabbed a nearby tree trunk, and kept her feet.

"Watch the hole there," she said coolly.

"It's not the hole I'm worried about," I said. "It's the snake a couple of inches from your hand."

She turned her head slowly to the left and then cautiously drew her hand back. "It's just a water snake," she pronounced. "They're mean but they aren't poisonous."

Another fifty yards of slogging through the swamp and I felt the ground rising. We came out somewhere not far from where we'd been before, but there was no sign of our tracks. We consulted our compasses again.

"North by northwest?" she asked. I nodded and we started into the foliage that covered most of the island.

Was he watching us now?

Then I told myself I was being histrionic, because, after all, our coming to the island was just a stab in the dark. The sheriff may have been right: Ben Picote might just as well have decided to run for home.

For that matter, he could have overturned in the river and drowned like the convicts. The convicts . . . They'd never been found. I was turning the thought over in my mind when Pepper, ahead of me, hacked a final vine with her machete and uttered a sigh of satisfaction.

I saw the river through the trees.

Still brown and menacing, with monsters in its depths.

We came out just below the spot where we'd found Absalom's body. Tracks showed where the posse had come with its ATVs and there was a muddle of boot prints in the sand. We walked north, up the bank, toward where we'd camped. A bed of charred wood marked where our fire had been and I saw where Ben had run down to the water's edge, after us.

I turned to Pepper.

"So where do we start?"

"I don't know. But he's here, I can feel it."

"Good for you. I hope he's on the same wavelength."

Something moved in the corner of my eye, far out on the river. It was a tug pushing a row of barges, and I turned to watch. Was she right? Was Ben really here? Or was he miles away? Even worse, was he somewhere *out there*, twisting in the muddy depths?

I started toward the head of the island, where we'd found our own boat. Pepper Courtney wasn't the only one with feelings: I'd had an odd sensation ever since we crossed the swamp. A feeling that told me we were very close to death.

The waves created by the passing barges rippled in and slopped against the sand. I saw the fallen tree ahead and willed myself to keep walking, because the feeling was stronger now and I didn't know if I was prepared for what I might find.

A wave lapped over the tree and something rose and fell on the other side. My heart stopped, but I made my feet keep going.

It had been something brown, like the tree itself, and when I got there I saw what it was: A flat bottomed boat, with a motor lashed firmly to the tree.

The boat Ben Picote had stolen.

When I turned to tell Pepper I saw that she had halted twenty feet behind me, rooted in her tracks.

Because there, between us, a crude spear in one hand, was Ben.

"What do you want?" he rasped. Mud streaked his orange prison jumpsuit, and his underwear showed white through rips in the fabric. Alone, dirty and hungry, without the rifle, he appeared smaller than I remembered.

"You look like hell," I said. "Here, have some water."

I reached for my belt to get my canteen, and the home-made spear lowered, toward my gut, but when he saw me unhooking the bottle, he relaxed the weapon. I tossed him the canteen and he caught it with one hand. Eyes going from one of us to the other, he unscrewed the cap and then, as if he couldn't help himself, raised the canteen and greedily drank.

Pepper glanced at me and gave a little nod. Ben lowered the canteen and wiped his mouth on a sleeve.

"Why did you come here?" he asked. "Are you with the law?"

"We came here to help you," Pepper said with all the guilelessness of a social worker, and I wondered how many times he'd heard that on the reservation.

But instead of a riposte, he just stared at her. Finally he said, "Thanks."

"The law isn't far behind, though," I broke in, letting my pack slide to the ground. "They'll work their way in this direction without our help. And they're not likely to read you your rights."

"He's right," Pepper agreed. "They'll shoot first and ask questions later. You've really got to give yourself up."

"Is that why you came here?" he asked, taking another sip. "To get me to go back?"

"To get you to keep from being killed," I said. "She's right, you know: They won't ask you nicely. They'll fill you full of holes and drag you back to town by the heels."

He sat down suddenly, as if his legs had gone out from under him, and closed his eyes for a long second.

"Why do you care?" he asked in a voice barely above a whisper.

"Because you're innocent," Pepper said. "We know you didn't kill anybody."

"No? Maybe I did. Maybe I found that old man digging up one of the graves. I'd kill anybody for that."

"Maybe," I said. "But I don't think you *did* find him

doing that. I think you're as much in the dark as we are about where he was getting those artifacts.''

"But I can say I killed him for disturbing the graves," he persisted. "I can say that. And if they killed me then, it would mean something. It would mean I died with honor."

"Honor, huh?" I shook my head. "How many people you seen die violently, Ben? Any at all? I saw a lot of men die in Nam. They *all* had honor. And they're still dead. Believe me, there's no honor in death. Just *death* in death. You want that?"

He frowned, as if having trouble absorbing my words.

"It's better than letting them lock me up in a white man's prison and then stick a needle in me, like I'm some dog, being put to sleep."

"Oh, Christ, cut the drama," I said. "There aren't aggravating circumstances, so it wouldn't ever come to that even if you *were* convicted, which is damn unlikely. Even a blind lawyer could get you off unless they've got a hell of a lot more evidence than I've heard about. Just being on the same island as the dead man isn't proof you killed him." It sounded good as I said it, but I knew even as the words left my mouth that people had been convicted on less.

"I still don't know why you care," he said. "I shot at you. I tried to kill you when you left."

I sighed. "If you'd tried to kill us we'd be dead. We're here because we're crazy. How's that for an excuse? We don't want to see some kid playing Geronimo find out too late that it's not a game."

"I'm not a kid," he protested. "At my age, in the old days, a boy was considered a man."

"Right. But that was then and this is now. Oh, goddamn it, Ben, stop being obstinate. You made your point. Now let's get you out of this mess."

Ben looked over at Pepper.

"He's right," she said. "We'll do everything we can to help you. We'll talk to the sheriff. We'll hire a lawyer . . ."

I flinched as I visualized some shyster attaching my house as payment for defending his client on death row.

But for a second I thought she'd scored. Then he shook his head.

"No. I'll stay here."

"Mind telling us why?" I asked.

"You wouldn't understand. It's just that here I can feel them all around, the ones who used to walk this land, the old ones, my ancestors. They've been talking to me all along. Do you think that's crazy?"

"I've got no problem with a vision quest. But the quest is over."

He shook his head again. "No. It goes on. The voices tell me what to do, and they're telling me to stay here, with them. If I die here, then I'll join them. *This* is our land, not that reservation across the river. *This* is where we belong. *This* is where I mean to stay."

I took a step toward him. "Ben . . ."

The spear came down, the point inches from my midsection.

"I don't want to hurt you," he said, "but I will if you don't go."

Pepper's hands balled into fists and I could sense her frustration.

"Get into the boat," Ben ordered. "I don't need it anymore. Get in the boat and leave this place. Leave me with the ancestors."

"Well, shit," I said. "Come on, Pepper."

"You're leaving?" she asked, incredulous.

"Got a better idea?"

I saw her expression twist into a mask of disgust.

"How about my canteen?" I asked him. "Mind giving it back?"

He reached down and handed it toward me. As his hand came forward I drew my own back slightly, making him extend himself, and then, without warning, I reached out, grabbed his wrist, and pulled him forward. He dropped the spear and lashed out with his other hand, catching me a glancing blow to the head, but I managed to twist his arm behind him, and then we toppled forward onto the sand.

He thrashed under me but I outweighed him and kept my body against his.

"My pack," I yelled to Pepper. "There's a rope in it."

She hesitated a second, then made her decision. She reached into my knapsack and came out with a length of nylon cord.

"Here," I called and grabbed it with one hand.

"Goddamn it, let me go," Ben shouted.

"Here," I yelled to Pepper. "He's too lively for me. You'll have to tie him."

"Are you sure?"

"Can you think of any other way to get him back to town without killing him?"

She looped the rope around one of Ben's wrists.

"I'll kill you," Ben promised.

"No, you won't," I said. "Tie it, quick."

She drew the loop tight and then slipped another length around the other wrist.

She pulled and all of a sudden, as if sensing the effort was no longer worth it, he gave up. I rolled off him and saw him turn his head away, and I realized he must be crying. I took the rope and made a few more loops around his arms and then dragged him to a sitting position. He buried his head in his chest.

"You'll have to carry me," he threatened. "I won't walk."

I looked over at the little boat. If we could make it upstream to the ferry landing at St. Francisville there would be people there to help.

"Have it your way," I said. I knotted the rope and then hoisted him half-upright. "Give me a hand," I told Pepper. "We'll load him in the boat."

She helped me drag him to the vessel. I pulled it up onto the sand and then wrestled him inside, to the center, and motioned for Pepper to help me push it back into the water and maneuver it around parallel to shore.

All the while he lay unmoving in the bottom and I thought I understood now what was going on: He didn't really want to die, just to be able to tell himself he'd done all he could. Well, we'd made it possible for him to feel good about himself, but now I was feeling very old and tired.

I stepped into the stern and Pepper handed me my pack.

The outboard was an old Evinrude 25 and I didn't know how much gas it had left.

The boat rocked as Pepper got in. I pulled the cord. The engine sputtered, but on the third pull it caught and I nosed the craft out into the stream.

The first twenty minutes were uneventful. The wind whipped my face, a hot breath filled with the smell of oil and mud. The shore passed agonizingly slowly and I tried to calculate our progress: By my reckoning we hadn't gone more than a half-mile, staying between the powerful current on the left and the snags and shoals of the shore on our right. The engine probably hadn't been full when Ben had stolen the boat. He hadn't used much fuel coming downstream, but there still couldn't be much left in the tank.

I cast a leery eye at the woods and swamps on our right and saw the little trail where we'd put in a few days ago. It would be a long walk out with a captive but it was better than drifting . . . All of a sudden my idea of going upstream to St. Francisville didn't seem like a very good one at all.

I looked down at Ben. He lay motionless in the center of the hull, his eyes on my face. He mouthed something but it was lost in the noise of the motor. Pepper pointed at something ahead and I saw that we were coming up on a high bluff, the first of the hills that marked the end of the floodplain. The river made a slight curve here, cutting into the side of the promontory and I felt the increased velocity as the little boat fought the current, coming almost to a halt.

Maybe, I thought, I should steer out further into the river, try to get around this current, but I discarded the idea almost as soon as I had it: If the engine quit then, we'd be at the mercy of forces we could never control. Pepper was still pointing, yelling something back at me, and I realized she was indicating something on the top of the bluff. I looked up and blinked.

Something metallic flashed in my eyes.

Ben saw it now, twisting around.

The flash gave way to an outline, a man silhouetted against the sky. He had something long and sticklike in his hand, and he was pointing it in our direction.

Ben sat up suddenly and I realized why he'd been so quiet: He'd been slipping out of his bonds and now he raised a hand, as if to shield himself, but it was too late.

The bullet hit him in the midsection and I heard him grunt at the same time I heard the explosion. He rocked back, his hands flying up, and I jerked the tiller left, to get us onto the shore.

It was too late: Ben was standing now, rocking the boat from side to side, and the next bullet hit him in the shoulder, spinning him around and causing his body to fall left, against the side of the boat.

The little craft went over, and I gulped a mouthful of muddy water. Wetness surrounded me and something under the surface struck my leg. I grabbed for the side of the hull and felt my hand grip the edge. Ben was gone now, swept away by the current, but I saw Pepper a few feet away, arms flailing in the air. I reached out, caught her hand with my free one, and pulled.

For a terrifying second our eyes met and then her hand let go and the waters took her away.

TWENTY-FOUR

When I opened my eyes I was staring into the sun. The bottom half of my body floated, rising and falling on unseen currents. A fly buzzed near my ear, and I turned my head. There was tall grass on my left and above it, trees.

I rolled onto my side and started to cough. Water trickled out of my mouth and with it the remains of my noon meal. When I finished retching I hoisted myself onto my hands and knees and looked around.

My legs were in the water and my hands were invisible in a sea of mud. I tugged my arms loose and dragged myself forward, into the grass and out of the water.

I had no idea where I was. Someone had shot at us, that much I vaguely remembered, and then I remembered the sucking waters and the terrible feeling as Pepper's hand jerked away from my own.

Gone. She and Ben were both gone and only I was left. I don't think it sunk in.

The sun was still hot but it was already low in the sky. Another hour or two and dusk would fall.

I hauled myself to my feet and stood swaying on the river's edge, trying to orient myself. What bank was I on? The current was flowing from my right to my left. So I'd beached on the same side we'd been on when the sniper had struck.

But how far downstream was I?

I craned my head, trying to look out over the water, but I was in a slight, convex bend, so that each end was blinded by vegetation. I could be a few feet from where we'd capsized, or a mile. I turned and took a step forward, my brain telling me I had to find a way out, and then my legs gave way and I toppled forward, into the brush.

For a long time I looked down at the baked mud, my eyes following the cracks. I was alive, but what did it matter? I fought an overwhelming urge to close my eyes and slump forward.

Then I heard branches breaking.

Something was in the brush above.

The trouble was I didn't have the energy to fight it.

Probably the man with the rifle. He'd find me here and then it would be over.

"Come on," I croaked. "Get it done."

The movement stopped, and then I heard a rushing of steps.

I raised my eyes to the forest and saw movement.

The vines parted and Pepper lurched out.

She looked like a mudhead kachina, slathered over with gray gumbo, her straw hat replaced by a nest of dried mud and leaves.

"Alan!" she cried out, and I thought she'd never looked better.

I scrambled back to my feet and lurched toward her.

"My God, I thought you were dead," I blurted.

"Same here," she said and grabbed my hands with both of hers. For a brief second we embraced and then drew away, mutually, as if we'd shocked each other.

She sat down then and I saw deep scratches on her arms and streaks on her face.

"I've been wandering along the bank," she mumbled. "I kept telling myself there was a chance that you might have made it . . ."

"And you were right."

"I wonder if there's a chance for Ben," she said.

I shook my head. "He took one bullet in the midsection and then another one in the arm or leg. If they didn't kill him he must have drowned."

"But who?"

I shook my head. "Somebody who feels threatened by our being out here."

I thought of the silhouette atop the bluff. I couldn't see the face or even get a good notion of the body size; all I knew was it was a man—or someone in a man's clothes.

"There's only one person that's got any stake in this," she said. "Your friend Willie Dupont."

"Isn't there another?" I asked.

The sound of the motor cut off her reply.

It was an outboard, coming upstream, on our side of the river. The noise grew louder and as we waited it emerged from the trees on the left, skimming against the current, thirty feet from shore. A lone figure hunched over the tiller, baseball cap shading the face.

Pepper raised an arm to wave and then, before I could say anything, dropped it. We were thinking the same thing, of course: What if it was the killer?

We watched the motorboat round the bend. Five minutes later the sound of the engine had died away.

"Well," she said. "What do we do now?"

"You don't have a plan?"

"Not at the moment."

I managed a smile. "That man in the boat was going somewhere. We could toss a coin but I say let's go upstream."

"And if he was the killer?"

"Then we'll have to watch ourselves, won't we?"

"Alan, listen, about all the trouble I've given you . . ."

"That way," I said, pointing.

We started along the beach, trying to keep on the dried mud strip between the thick grass and the plastic goo at water's edge. Logs barred our way, and every time I climbed over one I felt more strength drain away. We came to the end of the bend and I stopped. Ahead was a bluff, jutting out over the water. Even from this angle it was unmistakable: It was the cliff on which our attacker had stood. The river had swept us only a couple of hundred yards downstream.

I stood motionless, waiting for a figure to appear against the sky, but there was none.

"Maybe he's gone," Pepper whispered.

"And if he isn't?" I looked around for a path and she pointed to a breach in the forest. There was a narrow game trail and we followed it, ducking into the protective darkness of the woods.

We had to climb to the top of the bluff, because if someone had been there, that meant there might be a road, and a road meant a way out. Unless he was still there, waiting.

Fifty steps into the woods I saw a rise to our left and motioned to her. We trudged upward, trying to ignore the thorns and vines. The bluff was a relict ridge, poking out into the floodplain from the hills at its back, with the river eating away its base. Eventually the river would claim it all, but not quite yet.

I paused, panting, and wiped the sweat off my face with an arm. What if we were wrong and there was no road above, no trail of any kind? What if our attacker had just moored a boat there and climbed up to pick us off as we passed?

I took a deep breath and flailed away at the briars, managing to edge upward another two feet. Pieces of shirt and skin came off together and then I was free. I looked back for Pepper. She was taking a slightly different route, but I could tell it was no easier. I turned back to see what was in front of me.

High grass.

I blundered into it and ten feet on halted.

There was a clear space ahead, with no trees. I forced myself the rest of the way, and thirty seconds later I stood in a clearing. To my relief, I saw a faint vehicle track leading from the direction of the hills, on the right.

It was a way out.

I waited until Pepper was beside me.

"Let's check it out," I said. "You wait in the woods and I'll see if the coast is clear."

She shook her head. "No way. I've come this far."

Too tired to argue, I began to edge along the clearing, heading toward the river. Whoever had shot at us was probably gone now, but maybe we could find some shell casings as evidence.

The clearing was eerily still and the only noise was the muted wash of the river below. Even the birds were quiet, and as I scanned the yellow grass that stuck up in clumps, I had the sense of visiting a dead place.

The ground rose ahead of me, to the dropoff over the river, but there were some ruts before I got there, as if someone had spun his wheels in the earth. But there were too many ruts to have been made by a vehicle. And as I neared the spot, I saw that the scars weren't ruts at all.

"Alan," Pepper breathed from beside me and I turned involuntarily to look at her. She was trembling, like she was caught in a sudden blast of air, and when I reached out to reassure her I saw that my own hand was trembling, too.

The places where the earth had been turned up were more than ruts and even from where we stood, ten yards away, I could see something orange.

I fought the sickness churning my belly and made myself go closer. The orange was from Ben Picote's jumpsuit. He was lying beside a shallow grave, facedown.

I looked at the graves closer to the bluff: There were two that looked fresh, a matter of a few days at most, and I thought I knew who they belonged to.

Pepper pointed: "Are those the—?"

"Yeah," I said. "The two convicts."

"My God."

We walked past the fresh mounds to what appeared to be older interments. At one of them, a wild animal had been at work and a jaw gaped from the dirt. I stopped and picked up a shell necklace that had evidently been in the grave with the bones.

Pepper stared, transfixed. "This is the place," she said. "*Alan, this is the place.*"

I nodded, unsure whether to exult or run. As I walked I saw that there were bones all around, poking from the earth at odd angles—skulls, jawbones, femurs, ribs, even a pelvis. I tried to count but I lost track at forty. They were too jumbled to clearly distinguish. But one thing was sure: The graves themselves were strewn with the burial artifacts of the Tunica nation. A combination of erosion, wild animals, and someone with a spade had uprooted them from their earthen chambers, and now they lay white and bleached in the gold evening.

Pepper crossed her arms over her chest, as if to still the shivering, and I saw her shaking her head in amazement.

"I can't believe it," she mumbled. Then, suddenly, she stooped by the first skull and raised it with one hand.

"Alan, this can't be."

"What?"

She pointed to one of the teeth. "This skull has a filling. Alan, these can't be Indians at all."

I stared down at the tooth, trying to make sense of it.

And Chloe Messner's words came back at me:

The tooth is yellowed, completely different wear pattern than Joseph Dupont's premolars. I think it's been lying around somewhere for a long time.

I looked over at the two fresher graves and started to gag. I thought I understood now.

"You're right," I said finally. "It isn't an Indian."

A cloud passed over the sun and for a second I thought I was dizzy.

Too late, I realized it wasn't a cloud, but a large human figure, standing at the edge of the bluff. A man in a baseball cap, with a rifle. And the rifle was pointed at us.

▰▰TWENTY-FIVE

"So you didn't drown after all?" rasped a voice I recognized. "Too bad."

Marcus Briney walked slowly down the bluff toward us. "Now I'll have to dig a place for you like I did *him*."

Pepper's mouth moved silently and I thought for an instant she was going to scream, but instead she finally articulated a single word: "Why?"

Briney shrugged. "Because you know where this place is now. You've been here and you've seen. Just like the old nigger. Bastard was a danger to me, always poking around. I finally had to get rid of him."

"But why?" she asked again. "For the treasure?"

Briney spat on the ground. "Treasure? This junk? I seen what happened to that other poor son-of-a-bitch found a treasure, how they took it away from him. Naw, this crap don't mean nothing to me. It ain't nothin' but Indian beads."

I turned slowly to Pepper.

"It's the graveyard that he's trying to protect," I said and turned back to the other man: "My God, Briney, how many of them were there?"

Briney smiled a crooked smile and shrugged again. "Dunno. Lost count a long time ago. Not so many, though. Twenty-five, tops." He walked over to some of the older graves. "And the last one was while I was still at the prison. That's been five years." He looked down at a bleached fragment of scapula. "Otis, you wise-ass little

202

bastard, you shouldn't of never tried me like you did. Now look at you, all in little bitty pieces when you coulda left prison a free man after only ten years.'' He squinted up at us again. "And you know he was a *white* man, too?'' He shook his head. "I always gave the niggers more leeway, because they didn't know no better. But a white man? Wasn't no reason in the world for a white man to act the way some of 'em did. I always tried to help, too. I was fair. Everybody said that. Man did his work, didn't make trouble, I was his best friend. I've had cons call me after they got out, thank me for what I did. There's men out there with new lives because they used their time to learn something.'' He sighed. "But there was others just too damn ornery to learn anything at all. Those were the ones I brought here.''

The setting sun sent little red fires dancing in his eyes.

"I told 'em I was gonna help 'em ex-cape.'' He chuckled. "And they did: I put 'em in my car and brought 'em here.''

"Nobody ever missed them?'' Pepper asked.

"Some of 'em I wrote up as escapes, and the rest just died in prison. Back in them days, when I started, there wasn't the kind of recordkeeping they have now. A man really could disappear in Angola and never come out. Well, who the hell cared? We're not talking about people, for God's sake: We're talking about scum. Look, my father was killed in the breakout of '33. Those animals shot him down like a dog. And the parish wouldn't even pay for the trials. Do you think they deserve any mercy?''

"And the two convicts,'' I said. "You got them, too.''

"Sure. It was sort of an accident. I come up here a lot to talk to my boys. Otis, Big Red, Largo, and the others. I tell 'em I'm sorry I had to do this but I explain how it had to be and they understand. I was up here when I seen them two. Well, it was an easy shot. And I figure I did the state a favor.''

"A favor like killing T-Joe Dupont?'' I asked.

"That crazy old nigger give him a tooth and T-Joe come asking me about it, said there wasn't no Indian with fillings and he was going to the law. I tried to stop him but he took off in his truck, so I nailed him through the back window."

"I figured as much," I said. "But why did Carter Wascom alibi you? What do you have on him?"

"Carter?" Briney cackled. "He's got a thing. He likes young girls. When Eulalia grew up he started after other ones. Got into some trouble in Natchez, when he was home visiting his folks, right before Eulalia got sick. They bought him out of it but they shut him out after that."

"And you found out about it."

"Well, being assistant warden gets you certain law enforcement connections. I picked it up from a sheriff's deputy up there I knew."

"So you blackmailed him into selling you your place at half what it was worth."

"What was he gonna do with the land? Hell, it was a bargain: He didn't want Eulalia to know, and when he stirred up all this crap after she died, he didn't want anybody to know. Wouldn't help his case any, would it?"

"You killed the dog."

"Sort of a reminder to Carter."

"And Absalom?"

"Couldn't let the old bastard go on, digging stuff up and passing it out to who knows who. So I followed him up here." He shrugged. "I was going to bury him with the others, but he ran. I shot him and he went over the edge."

"And now it's our turn," I said, trying to keep him from hearing the fear in my voice.

"Hey, you people was coming right at me. How was I supposed to know you hadn't figured out this place was here? And him in his orange jail uniform. Any citizen's got a right to shoot an escapee on sight, I say."

Pepper shook her head, disbelieving. "But what about the artifacts? The beads and these brass bells and . . ."

"He's a smart man," I said. "Mr. Briney here figured that if he buried the bodies with Indian artifacts, anybody like old Absalom who dug them up would figure it was an Indian graveyard and they'd keep quiet."

Briney grinned again. "You're smart, too. I wish I didn't have to kill you, but you got to understand."

"Yeah," I said, trying to keep him from seeing me shake.

"Walk on to the edge of the bluff," Briney said in a suddenly soft voice, like he was coaxing a child. "Go ahead of me and I promise you won't feel a thing. It'll be over quick and then I'll come and talk to you, too."

"Just a minute," I said, trying to buy a delay. "Tell me, who was the first one you killed? Do you remember? Do you remember where he was buried?"

Briney frowned. " 'Course I do. It was a big dumb coon-ass named Dugas. Always mouthing off. I was just a regular guard, then. It was about the time all those guys cut their heels. See, I wasn't sure up until then. But when I saw how they was trying to get out of work, how far they'd go, my mind was made up. Yeah. Clint Dugas." He walked over to a spot about midway in the boneyard. "Old Clint would be about here, I reckon." He squinted up at me. "Why?"

"Just curious."

"Well, enough curiosity. Just march up to the bluff, okay? Don't make it any harder than it's got to be."

Pepper shot me a look from the corner of her eye and I tried to think of some way to delay the inevitable.

"Go on," he said, poking the rifle at me, "or I'll have to shoot you both right here. Starting with *her*."

My legs wobbled and I wondered if I'd be able to make it the whole twenty yards. There had to be something I could do, some way to stop him. We passed the graves of the two convicts and I shuddered. Soon our graves would look the same way, and years from now, if we were lucky, somebody would dig up our bones. Lucky?

We came to Ben's body and I halted.

"Mr. Briney . . ."

The gun barrel poked me in the back. "Keep going."

I took a step but then I realized Pepper hadn't moved.

"I'm not going another step," she said. "You're just going to have to shoot me here."

I turned in time to see the gun barrel shift away, toward her.

"If that's what you want," Briney said softly and cocked the hammer.

That was when Ben groaned.

"What in hell?" Briney's head jerked around. Without thinking, I rushed him, pushing him backward. He tripped over the wounded man and lost his footing. The rifle went off and the bullet flew past my head. I grabbed the barrel and pushed it to the side, away from us. But Briney kicked out, his boot catching me in the groin. I doubled in agony and felt myself crumpling to the ground. Briney disentangled himself from Ben, grabbed the rifle, and for an eternal instant I stared down the barrel.

Then there was a sound like a gong being struck and I saw the weapon fall away as its owner toppled to the ground. I looked up through tears to see Pepper standing over him with a shovel.

"A man shouldn't leave his tools lying around," she said. "It could be dangerous."

I tried to grin between clenched teeth.

"Take your time," she said. "I've got the rifle now. And if there's any permanent damage I may just shoot him where he lies."

She turned toward me, reaching out to help me up. And didn't see Briney rising to his knees behind her. I yelled but it didn't matter, because he was on his feet then, swaying, and before she could level the rifle he toppled backward and disappeared over the edge.

▰▰▰ EPILOGUE

It was two days later and I was sitting in the shade of a red oak with David Goldman, watching the excavation crew sweat in the afternoon sun. It wasn't my crew, but a group from the forensic anthropology program at the university, and I was just as glad. Frank LeMoine, the official representative of the Tunica-Biloxis, had been hovering all day, to make sure that the wrong bones weren't disturbed. Not to be out-hovered, Bertha Bomberg, from the Corps of Engineers, had taken the forensic team aside and lectured them on proper archaeological method. The coroner, a thin little man named Potts, had come out in the morning, taken one look at the confusion, and prudently driven back to St. Francisville and his medical practice. No mixing in bureaucratic snafus for him.

By two o'clock the sun was at its zenith and Frank decided the spirits of the dead did not require that their descendants suffer sunstroke, so he drifted over to the hickory tree on the other side of the clearing and pulled the bill of his cap down over his face. From the corner of my eye I saw Bertha heave a sigh of relief and sneak over to her government carryall.

"So how did you figure it out?" David asked finally, waving away a fly. "I mean, that real Indian burials were there, too?"

"I saw a lot of bones," I said. "More than any twenty-five or thirty graves. I asked Briney where the first person he killed was buried. He pointed to a spot right in the mid-

207

dle. I'd looked at the ones on either side. There was a jawbone on the surface, just left of the Dugas grave. It didn't have any fillings."

"Son-of-a-bitch," David breathed. "You're smarter than you look."

"Tell P. E. Courtney," I said, my eyes fixed on one of the female diggers, who was at that moment on all fours in the boiling sun, probing the earth with a tiny dental pick.

David shook his head. "Women."

Oddly, I felt sorry for her. She'd come south looking for her brother and so far she hadn't had any luck. I wondered if she'd stay, and I felt a perverse wish that she would.

"Anyway," I went on, "I think Briney stumbled onto the lost village and its cemetery. I don't know if he realized it was the lost village or not, but he knew it would be a good place to bury his victims. If he just redistributed the beads and bells and other artifacts a little, a careless glance would make anybody who wasn't an expert figure they were part of the Indian burial ground, too."

"And old Absalom found it on his own, years later."

"That's how I make it. He was scrounging artifacts from the burials. The same burials Briney was borrowing artifacts from to deck out his own victims when he buried them alongside the dead Tunicas. That's why Briney had to get rid of him. He wasn't too much of a danger at first, but once people started asking Absalom to show them where it was, well . . ."

"And it wasn't on T-Joe's land or Carter Wascom's, either."

"No. Carter will just have to go on living with the ghost of Eulalia and worrying about the scum in the bayou."

"Any idea where it's coming from?"

I shrugged. "Somebody may have dumped some barrels illegally. Or it may be some other industry upstream, like a sawmill."

There was the sound of an engine behind us and I turned my head in time to see a white car with the Public Safety and Corrections logo struggling up the incline. It gave up halfway there, its tires spitting dirt, and finally the driver shut off the engine. The doors opened and Warden Goo-

deau and two men I didn't know got out. One of them had
the air-brushed good looks of a politician and the other was
younger and carried a camera. Goodeau puffed uphill toward us, and I heard a car door slam on the other side of
the clearing. Bertha had seen them and was taking the short
way, dodging through the diggers, determined to be first.
But Frank was no slouch. At the first sound he'd jumped
to his feet and had a good ten yards on her. Levi Goodeau
stopped when he got to David and me and shook hands.

"How's it going?" he asked.

"You'll have to ask them," I said, shaking his hand.
"We're just observers."

"And glad of it," David mumbled, forcing himself up
despite his cast.

"This is Mr. Cromwell," Goodeau said. "Secretary of
the Department of Public Safety and Corrections."

Cromwell stuck out a hand and gave us the old "vote
for me" smile. "Glad to meetcha," he said. "You fellas
did a fine job."

The administration that employed him had only been in
office two years, so he could afford to congratulate us.

"This is Bud Wiley from the newspaper. He wants to
take a few pictures."

By that time Frank LeMoine had reached us. "You
aren't going to photograph the dead?" he demanded.

Before anyone could answer, Bertha had shoved past
him:

"I'm with the Corps of Engineers, in charge here. Can
I help you gentlemen?"

"I don't want them taking pictures of our people's dead
bodies," Frank said flatly.

"Well, could we just get a shot of the crew digging?"
Cromwell asked.

"The Corps of Engineers has to give permission for any
photographs not taken as part of the official archaeological
investigation," Bertha declared.

Cromwell put his arms over each of their shoulders and
the trio walked into the sun, the photographer trailing. I
saw them whispering to one another, saw Frank start to pull

away, saw Cromwell nod, then Bertha raise an arm in indignation.

"What a train wreck," David muttered. "Everybody's got to be in charge."

Warden Goodeau gave a little chuckle. "Human nature, I guess." Then his face lit with his optimist's smile. "But it could've turned out worse. I mean, the Indian boy is going to be all right. I visited him in the hospital this morning."

"There's that," I said.

"But it doesn't do much for the image of the prison. Granted, it happened before I was there and before Mr. Cromwell was secretary. But people won't remember who was who. All they'll remember is that Angola was the place where all those inmates were killed." He shook his head. "It'll take a long time to live down."

I nodded silently. He was right.

"Well, we'll see they get a decent burial," he said. "That's the least we can do. I guess they're just going to leave the Indians there?"

"That's the plan for now," I said. But I knew, as we all did, that the river was slowly eating away the base of the bluff, and that before much longer all the bones would be in the river. "The Tunica will probably decide to rebury them. There's a special state commission that makes those kinds of decisions."

"Right," David snorted. "If they can get a quorum together."

Actually, I thought, Marvin Ghecko had done a fairly good job of wending his way between the Scylla and Charybdis of Native American sensitivities and bureaucratic red tape, so that the forensic team could unearth the recent victims while a member of the tribe was on hand to see that the true ancients were not disturbed.

"Briney . . ." Goodeau breathed, and I knew what he was thinking: The man had vanished. We all assumed he was dead but who could say?

The photographer was backing off from the excavators now, his camera to his eye, and it was with a shock that I realized he was backing toward the spot from which Briney had fallen. Well, no one said journalism was risk-free. I relaxed and waited to see what would happen. I saw that Mr. Cromwell had taken a pose among the forensic team, presumably as titular head of the State Police, and, while Bomberg and LeMoine were beside him, I had a feeling the camera would somehow cut them out.

Then one of the excavators got up from her hands and knees and started toward us, and I saw Cromwell's head turn toward her in disbelief.

"Enough of that crap," Pepper said, joining us in the shade. "He can get his own stooges for PR shots."

David's head gave a little jerk in her direction, and I realized she'd taken on new stature in his eyes.

"How you feeling?" she asked me.

"A little sore," I said.

She nodded. "I imagine so, where he hit you."

I coughed.

"I've been meaning to tell you how well I think you handled things," she said suddenly. "Everything from Ben to Briney himself."

"Ben's just a crazy kid," I said. "As for Briney, I was scared to death."

"Yeah, but you'd been scared before, so you had practice." She saw my frown. "You know, from Vietnam."

"I wasn't in Nam," I said. "I just said that to make my point with Ben. Truth is, I couldn't think of anything else to say."

Pepper's mouth came partway open, then closed.

"You're full of surprises," she said.

"I try," I said modestly.

We were still staring at each other when we heard an outcry from the direction of the excavation. Pepper turned and Goodeau shaded his eyes with a hand. The photographer was on his hands and knees now, on the edge of the precipice, and for a minute I had the absurd notion that he was polishing Cromwell's shoes. By now the diggers had risen from their holes, and even Bomberg and LeMoine had gone to the edge of the bluff.

Goodeau started forward, Pepper at his side, and even David hobbled after them on his crutch, but I didn't want to go, because I had a premonition and it did funny things to my stomach. As I got to the excavations, I saw Bomberg turn away from the edge, a strange, green tint to her face.

"Oh, my God," she mumbled and headed for the bushes.

"I just dropped my lens cap," the photographer sputtered. "I was looking for it in the dirt when I saw it, I didn't know, I mean, it was an accident . . ." He seemed to think I deserved an explanation but I ignored him. Ahead of me, Cromwell was wiping his handsome face with a handkerchief, and I thought I saw his hand shaking.

"Need a boat," Frank LeMoine pronounced, walking away. "Can't do anything from here but fall in with him."

And I knew my premonition was correct.

Goodeau and Pepper were both staring down when I reached them.

"Better not get too close," I said.

Goodeau nodded and stepped back, but Pepper stayed rooted.

"Alan, look, down there." Her hand came out and grabbed my arm, as if I were a lifeline. "It's him."

I didn't have to look down, but I did, anyway, and what I saw was a man's body, caught in the roots of an upended tree, turning and bobbing with the current. The fish and turtles had eaten away part of the flesh, so that the white of his skull showed where his face had been, but the clothes told the story: It was Marcus Briney.

I stared for a long time, until I felt her grip relax, and then we turned away together.

"Well, I'll call for a boat," Warden Goodeau said under his breath. Frank LeMoine had gone back to sit under the tree and I knew what he was thinking: This one isn't one of ours. It's one of theirs. *And it's the one who did the damage, so the case has come full circle, and now the old ones can sleep.*

Sleep. Suddenly it sounded pretty good to me, too.

"Alan, are you all right?"

I jerked my head up at her voice.

"Me? I'm fine."

"That's good. Because all at once I'm so tired I can hardly stand up."

"I could take you back," I said.

She nodded slowly. "I think I'd like that. If you wouldn't mind."

We started down the slope together to where I was parked.

"David can catch a ride back with some of the crew," I said. "I'll go tell him."

She nodded.

I told David I was taking her home. At first he protested, then gave a shrug. "Why not? The fresh air feels good after all that time in the hospital."

I nodded and we started toward the car. So I'd handled it well. An accolade. From P. E. Courtney, Ph.D., no less. My limbs already felt lighter, and some of the fatigue of the last few days began to lift.

"Look," I said, just before we got to the Blazer. "About what you said up there after Briney hit me, about if I had permanent damage—"

She gave me a blank look. "I don't know what you're talking about."

I let her open her own door and then I got in and drove her home.

Nationally Bestselling Author

J·A·JANCE

The J.P. Beaumont Mysteries

TAUT, SUSPENSEFUL MYSTERIES
BY *NEW YORK TIMES*
BESTSELLING AUTHOR

PATRICIA CORNWELL

Featuring Kay Scarpetta, M.E.

POSTMORTEM
71021-8/ $6.99 US/ $8.99 Can
"Taut, riveting—whatever your favorite strong adjective,
you'll use it about this book!"
Sara Paretsky

ALL THAT REMAINS
71833-2/ $6.99 US/ $8.99 Can
"Riveting...compelling...original..."
Cosmopolitan

BODY OF EVIDENCE
71701-8/ $6.99 US/ $8.99 Can

CRUEL AND UNUSUAL
71834-0/ $6.99 US/ $8.99 Can